A WISCONSIN CHRISTMAS ANTHOLOGY

a Wisconsin Christmas anthology

Edited by
Terry R. Engels

Partridge Press
St. Cloud, Minnesota

Cover Design: Ann Blattner
Editor: Theresa Rice Engels
Project Editor: Stephen E. Engels
Associate Editor: Sylvia Tiala
Original Art: Ethel Boyle
Typography: North Star Press of St. Cloud, Inc.

About the cover:
As a young man Milwaukee-born Artist Carl Von Marr studied in Germany. Christmas Eve, 1884, homesick for his family and friends in Wisconsin, Von Marr went out for a walk. While he was gone the woman who headed the household where he was staying decorated his room. Delighted by the tree and moved by her concern he painted this Christmas scene. The painting is part of the permanent collection of the Milwaukee Art Museum, a donation of Mrs. William Hughes Marshall. In December it often stood atop the entranceway to the galleries, festooned with holiday greens.

Partridge Press
P. O. Box 364
St. Cloud, Minnesota, 56302
612-253-1145

With special thanks to the State Historical Society, Madison; Sally Wood, assistant curator at the Old Wade House, Greenbush; staff of the Pendarvis Historic Site, Mineral Point and the Madeline Island Historic Museum; Alice Wendt of the Ozakee County Historical Society, Cedarburg; Sister Marie Lawrence, O.P., of the Convent Library, Sinsinawa; Joyce Allerman, Amy Breisch and Elda Schweisser of New Glarus; Barbara Antoine, Nancy Elrod, and Edward Allman of the American Club, Kohler; Staff of the Milwaukee County Historical Society, Milwaukee Public Library, Rice Lake Public Library, Eau Claire Public Library, Ashland Public Library, and the Platteville Public Library, State Heritage Room.

CONTENTS

SKATING, SLEIGH RIDES & SNOWFALL

EARLY CELEBRATIONS
Blackrobes, Voyageurs and Native Americans

JUST BEFORE CHRISTMAS

KEEPING CHRISTMAS THEN AND NOW

CHRISTMAS ON MAIN STREET

CHRISTMAS RECIPES

Newspaper Accounts of Christmas in Wisconsin: *Milwaukee Sentinel;*
Whitehall Register; Berlin Courant; Lake Mills Leader; Evening Times, Monroe;
Milwaukee Journal; Eau Claire Times; Kohler News.

The Skating Pond
Currier & Ives, 1860

SKATING SLEIGH RIDES & SNOWFALL

A Merry Christmas

How it was observed in Milwaukee

The report on Christmas observances of a festive nature will be brief as these were chiefly private. Suffice it that the day was heartily celebrated by all. Owing to the disappearance of the snow a few days ago the many delightful sleigh rides which had been fondly anticipated by the weaker and younger vessels had to be postponed and something else substituted. The principal amusement of the day was

SKATING AT UNION PARK

At this new and fashionable resort everything went favorably for the highest development of fun. The ice was "elegant" (we heard a very handsome young lady pronounce it so), the weather was just right, not windy, the attendance large and fashionable, the music stimulating, the park spacious, and—it was Christmas! Under all these circumstances it is no wonder that several thousand persons visited the park. There was also fancy skating by Mr. Sterling and a game of curling. The fun kept up in the park until ten o'clock in the evening.

The Sentinel, Milwaukee, December 26, 1866

Something About Skating

Tips from *The Register*, Whitewater, Wisconsin, December 27, 1861

Rule 1:
Avoid skates that are strapped on the feet, as they prevent the circulation, and the foot becomes frozen before the skater is aware of it.

Rule 2:
It's not so much the object to skate fast as to skate gracefully: and this is sooner and more easily learned by skating with deliberation.

Rule 3:
If the wind is blowing, a veil should be worn over the face, at least of ladies and children: otherwise a fatal inflamation of the lungs, "pneumonia," may take place.

Rule 4:
Never carry anything in the mouth while skating, nor any hard substance to the hand.

Rule 5:
If the thermometer is below zero, and the wind is blowing, no lady or child should be skating.

Rule 6:
Always keep your eyes about you, looking ahead and upward, not on the ice, that you may not run against some lady, or child or learner.

Rule 7:
The grace, exercise, and healthfulness of skating on ice, can be had, without any of its dangers, by the use of skates with rollers attached, on common floors; better if covered with oil-cloth.

Peck's Bad Boy at Christmas
His Pa Goes Skating
by George W. Peck

"What is that stuff on your shirt bosom, that looks like soap grease?" said the grocery man to the bad boy, as he came into the grocery the morning after Christmas.

The boy looked at his shirt front, put his fingers on the stuff and smelled of his fingers, and then said, "O, that is nothing but a little of the turkey dressing and gravy. You see after Pa and I got back from the roller skating rink yesterday, Pa was all broke up, and he couldn't carve the turkey, and I had to do it, and Pa sat in a stuffed chair with his head tied up and a pillow amongst his legs, and he kept complaining that I didn't do it right. Gol darn a turkey anyway. I should think they would make a turkey flat on the back, so he would lay on a greasy platter without skating all around the table. It looks easy to see Pa carve a turkey, but when I speared into the bosom of that turkey, and began to saw on it, the turkey rolled around as though it was on castors, and it was all that I could do to keep it out of Ma's lap. But I rassled with it till I got off enough white meat for Pa and Ma, and dark meat enough for me and I dug out the dressing, but most of it flew into my shirt bosom, cause the string that tied up the place where the dressing was concealed about the person of the turkey broke prematurely, and one oyster hit Pa in the eye, and he said I was as awkward as a cross-eyed girl trying to kiss a man with a hair lip. If I ever get to be the head of a family I shall carve turkeys with a corn sheller."

"But what broke your Pa up at the roller skating rink?" asked the grocery man.

"O, everything broke him up. He is split up so Ma buttons the top of his pants to his collar button, like a bicycle rider. Well, he had no business to have told me and my chum that he used to be the best skater in North America, when he was a boy. He said he skated once from Albany New York in an hour and eighty minutes. Me and my chum thought that if Pa was such a terror on skates we would get him to put on a pair of roller skates, and enter him as the 'great unknown,' and clean out the whole gang. We told Pa that he must remember that roller skates were different from ice skates, and that maybe he couldn't skate on them, but he said it didn't make any difference what they were as long as they were skates, and he would just paralyze the whole crowd. So we got a pair of big roller skates for him, and while we were strapping them on, Pa he looked at the skaters glide around on the smooth wax floor just as though they were greased. Pa looked at the skates on his feet, after they were fastened, sort of forlorn like, the way a horse thief does when they put shackles on his legs, and I told him if he was afraid he couldn't skate with them, we would take them off, but he said he would beat anybody that was there, or bust a suspender. Then we straightened Pa up and pointed him toward the middle of the room, and he said 'leggo,' and we just give him a little push to start him, and he began to go. Well, by gosh, you'd a died to have seen Pa try to stop. You see, you can't stick in your heel and stop, like you can on ice skates, and Pa soon found that out, and he began to turn sideways, and then he threw his arms and walked on his heels, and he lost his hat, and his eyes began to stick out, cause he was going right toward an iron post. One arm caught the post, and he circled around it a few times, and then he let go and began to fall, and sir, he kept falling all across the room, and everybody got out of the way, except a girl, and Pa grabbed her by the polonaise, like a drowning man grabs at straws, though there wasn't any straws in her polonaise as I know of, but Pa just pulled her along as though she was done up in shawl-strap, and his feet went out from under him and he struck on his shoulders and kept a going, with the girl dragging along like a bundle of clothes. If Pa had another pair of roller skates on his shoulders, and castors on his ears, he couldn't have slid along any better. Pa is a short, big man, and as he was rolling along on his back, he looked like a sofa with castors on, being pushed across the room by a girl. Finally Pa came to the wall and had to stop, and the girl fell right across him with her roller skates in his neck, and she called him an old brute, and told him if he didn't let go of her polonaise she would murder him. Just then my chum and me got there, and we amputated Pa from the girl, and lifted him up and told him for heaven's sake to let us take off the skates, 'cause he couldn't skate any more than a cow, and Pa was mad and said for us to let him alone, and he could skate all right, and we let go, and he struck out again. Well, sir, I was ashamed. An old man like Pa ought to know better than to try to be a boy.

This last time Pa said he was going to spread himself, and if I am any judge of a big spread, he did spread himself. Somehow the skates had got turned around sideways on his feet; and his feet got to going in different directions, and Pa's feet were getting so far apart that I was afraid I would have two Pa's half the size, with one leg apiece."

"I guess it knocked the breath out of him, for he didn't speak for a few minutes, and then he wanted to go home, and we put him in a street car, and he laid down on the hay and rode home. O, the work we had to get Pa's clothes off. He had cricks in his back, and everywhere, and Ma was away to one of the neighbors, to look at the presents, and I had to put liniment on Pa, and I made a mistake and got a bottle of furniture polish, and put it on Pa and rubbed it in, and when Ma came home, Pa smelled like a coffin at a charity funeral and Ma said there was no way of getting that varnish off of Pa till it wore off. Pa says holidays are a condemned nuisance anyway. He will have to stay in the house all this week."

"You are pretty rough on the old man," said the grocery man, after he has been so kind to you and given you nice presents."

"Nice presents nothing. All I got was a 'Come to Jesus' Christmas card, with brindle fringe, from Ma, and Pa gave me a pair of his old suspenders, and a calender with mottoes for every month, some quotations from scripture, such as 'Honor they father and thy mother,' and 'Evil communications corrupt two in a bush,' and 'A bird in the hand beats two pair.' Such things don't help a boy to be good. What a boy wants is club skates, and seven shot revolvers, and such things. Well, I must go and help Pa roll over in bed, and put on a new porous plaster. Good-bye."

> George W. Peck was a publisher and politician who served as mayor of Milwaukee and governor of Wisconsin. He had considerable reputation as a humorist, chiefly because of his series of *Peck's Bad Boy* stories.

The hills were white with the Christmas season when I came home. The frozen lagoons of Lake Wingra spiraled through the reeds brittle with frost, and from the tips of their leaves the snow fell in feathery clumps as we brushed them in swinging by on our skates. Meta and I left the narrow channel and headed out into the lake, a keen wind cutting our faces and whipping the snow across the clear spaces on the ice in delicate, fan-like runnels. There were many people on the lake, and many friends—good friends to whom we had clung and who had clung to us in the year of the storm. And now the dark robes of foreboding had fallen away from all of us, leaving us exulting in a fresh vitality almost giddying in its intensity.

We skated on the Four Lakes, we skiied down the steep slopes of Eagle Heights, and we walked on the frozen ruts and through highway drifts from village to village, stopping at the wayside hotels remembered from our wedding journey.

Ernest L. Meyer, *Hey Yellowback*

Sleigh Rides

by Lina Burkhardt Allmann

Sleigh rides. Who wouldn't enjoy a sleigh ride?

When I was growing up, it wasn't just fun that was the way we traveled in the winter time. There were different kinds of sleighs: bob-sleighs had four runners, two in front and two in the back. They usually had a box on them with seats to sit on. Some had planks for hauling logs and other uses on the farm. Then there was the cutter, with a single seat or two seats pulled by one horse or a team of horses. We had two bob-sleighs and one cutter. Our cutter was not a fancy one with a door on each side. Sometimes it was a very cold ride when the wind blew piling snow in big drifts. There were no snow plows to clear the roads. People had to shovel. If the snow banks were too high they drove around them, often through fields. Even after we had cars they could not be used on country roads until the roads were cleared of snow and ice, often not until spring.

If the snow on the road packed down unevenly, it caused sharp dips which were called pitch holes. At times, a cutter would tip over. If the horse was gentle she would stand still and wait until all was in place and you could go on. If the horse was nervous and easily excited, you were in trouble.

Sleigh ride parties were fun. Adults and teenagers enjoyed them as much as children. One year, our parents decided to give the children's choir from our church a sleigh ride to show their appreciation. Father drove to church where the children gathered after school anxiously waiting for the horses and sleigh to arrive. With blankets tucked around them, the ride to the farm was on its way. Some of those who lived in the city rarely had the opportunity for such an outing. When they arrived at the farm, they could play until supper was ready to be served. One little girl found an ear of corn; she came to mother asking what it was.

Mother's sister assisted with the serving. After supper and some singing, father took them back to church where their parents were waiting to take them home. It had been such an enjoyable time, it was repeated year after year. Once, when the roads were kept open by snow plows and scrapers, it wasn't possible to pull a sleigh over the bare ground. Then, the parents brought the children to the farm for the outing. Father would take them for rides through the woods and over fields. Nineteen forty-five was the last sleigh ride party for the children's choir. One of the horses had died, the other one was sold. A tractor took their place for the work on the farm.

Those days have not been forgotten. Occasionally, I have met someone who had been with those groups. They still remember and speak of that time, how much they enjoyed those sleigh rides when they were members of the children's choir.

* * * * *

The sleighing is now reported to be superb and when the mercury rises about twenty degrees we may look for a general clatter and jingling of sleigh bells. Every conceivable description of vehicle will be brought into requisition, and every horse will be made to perform prodigies of fleet traveling.

Whitewater Register, 1861

Sleighing to the Christmas Program
Gladys M. Rebelein

Twilight deepened into darkness on a December afternoon, and the last few snowflakes fluttered to the farmyard. My father smiled, "It is always good to have a little more snow, to insure good sleighing all winter." "Hurry with the chores," we do not want to be late for the Christmas program."

We children didn't need any reminder. Hadn't we practiced our songs and recitations every Sunday after Sunday School? Hadn't we stood still, or at least tried, while Mother patiently fitted our new clothes? Those Christmas clothes were something very special. One wore them first to the program, and then every Sunday until Easter. Last year's Christmas dress became a school dress to be worn every day, with a pinafore apron over it, and changed as soon as one came home from school. We knew that, even now as we were talking, Mother was carrying from the closet all of our new clothes and laying them out on our beds. But there was no time for daydreaming. There were chores to be done.

We hurried through our supper of fried potatoes, cheese, sauce canned the previous summer, and some Christmas cookies. The dishes too were washed quickly. We checked to be sure there was plenty of warm water in the reservoir of the old wood-and-coal-burning stove to wash ourselves with. Perhaps ears and necks were washed just a bit more carefully that night, but nevertheless, one basin of water had to be enough for all five of us. Water had to be carried by the pailful from the well, which was a long ways from the house, so it was used sparingly.

The sleigh had already been covered with a layer of straw that afternoon, and the horses had been harnessed, but not hitched. It was only a matter of minutes until the tugs were hooked to the bobsled and the neckyoke put in place. This was a special night so sleigh bells were strapped around each horse's belly.

Mom brought out the soapstone which had been heating in the oven and we two older children each carried out a horsehide robe. We children and Mom sat facing each other in the sleigh, our feet and legs crossing in the middle, each of us trying to get our feet nearer the soapstone. We placed the heavy robes across our laps.

Father, in his big sheepskin coat, stood at the front and drove the horses. If he became too chilled, he would clap his hands while holding the reins, or sometimes even jump out and run alongside the sleigh.

"Let's stop and pick up our cousins too," we yelled. "It will be fun." We all shoved together a little closer. The boys would have liked to show off a bit and run beside the sleigh, but our mothers forbade it on this night, when appearance was important.

The four miles to church were covered long before we had run out of chatter. Women and children were let out at the church door, while fathers drove their teams to the sheds in the parking lot. My father's shed was Number 22 and for that he paid a certain amount of rent each year. Once inside we took off our heavy coats and boots while our mothers tried to brush our hair a bit and straighten shirts and dresses, all the while secretly hoping that no restroom trips would be necessary before the program was over. The "restrooms" were way out beyond the horse sheds, and a trip there meant putting on coats and boots and going out into the dark.

Somehow each of us children managed to get through our part of the program without too many mistakes. We felt special in our new clothes. The sparkle of excitement in the eyes of the very little children was almost brighter than the candles lighting the huge tree. Then it was gift time. There was a sack filled with Christmas goodies for each of us, and a gift under the tree from our Sunday School teacher, and maybe even a present from a cousin or a friend.

Finally it was all over, the Christmas hymns, the blessing, the final "Merry Christmas" called out to friends as sleighs departed. The sleigh was cold and so was the straw, and the soapstone had long since ceased to give out warmth. But it didn't matter. Our hearts were warm and gay, and only the littlest went to sleep.

* * * * *

In the winter the lumber wagon box was put on a pair of bobsleds. The box was filled almost half full with clean straw, and blankets were laid on top of that. We would sit right down on it, and it was both soft and warm. There were wool quilts over our laps, since we had no fur robes in the early days. Those horses clipped along at a good pace, and we enjoyed a fast ride. In winter the horses had bells on—some strings that reached all around their bellies. Every string had an individual sound. When another team would be coming toward us down the road, we could hear the bells at least half a mile away, and we knew who was coming by the sound. The horses did not have much exercise in winter, so when they had a chance to go, they surely could caper, and the bells would ring and jingle every minute. It was all the driver could do sometimes to keep them from running away. They would prance and jump and gallop for quite a way before they calmed down. We children dearly loved these sleigh rides.

My parents always kept those sleighbells. When I was married and lived in Oshkosh, sometimes I would hear those bells outside the house and go nearly wild with joy, for I could tell whose they were, and know my folks were there.

Thurine Oleson, *Wisconsin, My Home*

Winter in the Fox River Valley
by John Muir

In winter father came to the foot of the stairs and called us at six o'clock to feed the horses and cattle, grind axes, bring in wood, and do any other chores required, then breakfast, and out to work in the mealy, frosty snow by daybreak, chopping, fencing, etc. So in general our winter work was about as restless and trying as that of the long-day summer. No matter what the weather, there was always something to do. During heavy rains or snowstorms we worked in the barn, shelling corn, fanning wheat, thrashing with the flail, making axe-handles or ox-yokes, mending things, or sprouting and sorting potatoes in the cellar.

No pains were taken to diminish or in any way soften the natural hardships of this pioneer farm life; nor did any of the Europeans seem to know how to find reasonable ease and comfort if they would. The very best oak and hickory fuel was embarrassingly abundant and cost nothing but cutting and common sense; but instead of hauling great heart-cheering loads of it for wide, open, all-welcoming, climate-changing, beauty-making, Godlike ingle-fires, it was hauled with weary heart-breaking industry into fences and waste places to get it out of the way of the plough, and out of the way of doing good. The only fire for the whole house was the kitchen stove, with a fire-box about eighteen inches long and eight inches wide and deep—scant space for three or four small sticks, around which in hard zero weather all the family of ten persons shivered, and beneath which in the morning we found our socks and coarse, soggy boots frozen solid. We were not allowed to start even this despicable little fire in its black box to thaw them. No, we had to squeeze our throbbing, aching, chilblained feet into them, causing greater pain than toothache, and hurry out to chores. Fortunately the miserable chilblain pain began to abate as soon as the temperature of our feet approached the freezing-point, enabling us in spite of hard work and hard frost to enjoy the winter beauty— the wonderful radiance of the snow when it was starry with crystals, and the dawns and the sunsets and white noons, and the cheery, enlivening company of the brave chickadees and nuthatches.

The winter stars far surpassed those of our stormy Scotland in brightness, and we gazed and gazed as though we had never seen stars before. Oftentimes the heavens were made still more glorious by auroras, the long lance rays, called "Merry Dancers" in Scotland, streaming with startling tremulous motion to the zenith. Usually the electric auroral light is white or pale yellow, but in the third or fourth of our Wisconsin winters there was a magnificently colored aurora that was seen and admired over nearly all the continent. The whole sky was draped in graceful purple and crimson folds glorious beyond description. Father called us out into the yard in front of the house where we had a wide view, crying, "Come! Come, mother! Come, bairns! and see the glory of God. All the sky is clad in a robe of red light. Look straight up to the crown where the folds are gathered. Hush and wonder and adore, for surely this is the clothing of the Lord Himself, and perhaps He will even now appear looking down from his high heaven." This celestial show was far more glorious than anything we had ever yet beheld, and throughout that wonderful winter hardly anything else was spoken of.

John Muir is often called the founder of the American conservation movement. In 1849 at the age eleven, he came to America from Scotland with his family. They settled as did many other Scotch, Irish, and English, along the Fox River. He relates these difficult but wonderful pioneer years in The Story of My Boyhood and Youth. *His understanding of and appreciation for nature was fostered in his Wisconsin boyhood.*

Snowfall in Childhood

by Ben Hecht

I got out of bed to see what had happened in the night. I was thirteen years old. I had fallen asleep watching the snow falling through the half-frosted window.

But though the snow had promised to keep falling for a long time, perhaps three or four days, on opening my eyes I was full of doubts. Snowstorms usually ended too soon.

While getting out of bed I remembered how, as I was nearly asleep, the night outside the frosted window had seemed to burst into a white jungle. I had dreamed of streets and houses buried in snow.

I hurried barefooted to the window. It was scribbled with a thick frost and I couldn't see through it. The room was cold and through the open window came the fresh smell of snow like the moist nose of an animal resting on the ledge and breathing into the room.

I knew from the smell and the darkness of the window that snow was falling. I melted a peephole on the glass with my palms. I saw that this time the snow had not fooled me. There it was, still coming down white and silent and too thick for the wind to move, and the trees and houses were almost as I had dreamed. I watched, shivering and happy. Then I dressed, pulling on my clothes as if the house were on fire. I was finished with breakfast and out in the storm two hours before school time.

The world had changed. All the houses, fences, and barren trees had new shapes. Everything was round and white and un-familiar.

I set out through these new streets on a voyage of discovery. The unknown surrounded me. Through the thick falling snow, the trees, houses and fences looked like ghost shapes that had floated down out of the sky during the night. The morning was without light, but the snowfall hung and swayed like a marvelous lantern over the streets. The snowbanks, already over my head in places, glowed mysteriously.

I was pleased with this new world. It seemed to belong to me more than that other world which lay hidden.

I headed for the school, jumping like a clumsy rabbit in and out of snowbanks. It seemed wrong to spoil the smooth outlines of these snowdrifts and I hoped that nobody else would pass this way after me. In that case the thick falling snow would soon restore the damage. Reassured by this hope I continued on my devastations like some wanton explorer. I began to feel that no one would dare the dangers of my wake. Then, as I became more aware of the noble proportions of this snowstorm I stopped worrying altogether about the marring of this new and glowing world. Other snows had melted and been shoveled away, but this snow would never disappear. The sun would never shine again and the little Wisconsin town through which I plunged and tumbled to school on this dark storm-filled morning was from now on an arctic land full of danger and adventure.

When eventually, encased in snow, I arrived at the school, I found scores of white-covered figures already there. The girls had taken shelter inside, but the boys stayed in the storm. They jumped in and out of the snowdrifts and tumbled through the deep unbroken white fields in front of the school.

Muffled cries filled the street. Someone had discovered how far-away our voices sounded in the snowfall and this started the screaming. We screamed for ten minutes, delighted with the fact that our voices no longer carried and that the snowstorm had made us nearly dumb.

Tired with two hours of such plunging and rolling, I joined a number of boys who like myself had been busy since dawn and who now stood for the last few minutes before the school bell with half-frozen faces staring at the heavily falling snow as if it were some game they couldn't bear to leave.

Ben Hecht was born in 1894. He was brought up in Racine where he sailed Lake Michigan, studied the violin, and perfected an acrobatic act. After high school graduation he became a newspaper man in Chicago, and wrote numerous plays, novels, and short stories. For over forty years he was the most prolific and influential of Hollywood screenwriters; in fact he won the first Academy Award for Screenplay in 1929.

Long Journey Through Wisconsin Territory by Sleigh, 1837

by Father Samuel Mazzuchelli

The beautiful broad natural prairies of Wisconsin Territory usually offer the traveler in the cold season an easy and commodious passage over the snow which covers them with its white mantle for the space of many months. In February, 1837, the Missionary took advantage of this curious phase of nature to make a journey to Green Bay, two hundred and ten miles from Galena, his object being to recover some articles needed for the Church, stored there two years before. It is not easy to give an idea of a course of four hundred and twenty miles, all alone, across a country still unbroken and unsettled, in the very depth of winter severity, in a sledge drawn by a single horse, crossing prairies, woods, rivers, frozen lakes, over a road at times smooth and easily followed because marked by the tracks of many other vehicles, at other times hardly discernible because little used and hidden under the snow drifted there by the wind. It may be observed that in this part of the country the snow is seldom so deep as to render the road too hard or entirely impassable; so in winter the highways from one little village to another are generally well traced through the snow by the sledges of the wayfarers, while in the vast prairies the tracks do not remain plain and well-defined as in the woods, on account of the wind which blows there as it does over the sea, and carries with it the frozen snow like dust, obliterating in an instant the tracks just made. Many are the difficulties to be encountered by the inexperienced traveler; there are streams with high banks and of course with no bridge, whose waters fed by springs near, do not freeze over; the ice is not always solid upon the lakes and is very treacherous and dangerous on certain rivers; in the hollows of the undulating prairie the snow is often drifted by the wind in a mass to the depth of six or seven feet. The greatest, most dreaded peril on these vast prairies is caused by the falling snow, so as to completely cover the track, and shutting out the slightest view of the surroundings, even of east and west; desperate is the condition then of one who finds himself in such a strait when the fury of the freezing wind, with the dense, powdery snow, so confuses him that he loses his way and is forced in spite of himself to stop his horse under the stormy sky, and wait until the fury of the storm passes by. In these desperate straits many are found frozen to death. The prudent forethought which counts its steps before taking them, and prepares for possible dangers will ordinarily prevent misfortunes of this nature.

On the occasion of this journey, the Priest visited his Menominee Indians who were engaged in fishing at Lake Winnebago; great was the consolation and spiritual gladness he experienced seeing again those good Christians whom he had won but a few years before from the superstitions of the savage to the truths of the Gospel, and on their part his presence gave them the greatest delight. To sanctify such a meeting, forty-two of them received from his hands that Heavenly Bread which divinely unites hearts in the love of Jesus Christ. As he made his way towards his destination, he stopped at various stations to provide for the spiritual needs of the Catholics dispersed throughout the western part of the Territory. He who bears the word of Truth should imitate his Divine Master, Who went about doing good, lightening the burdens of the heavy-laden and sore oppressed.

Fox River Plum Pudding

The Fox River Valley was home, in addition to John Muir, to many others of English, Irish, and Scotch descent. Christmas in the British tradition would not be Christmas without plum pudding, or as the Cornish from Mineral Point called it, suet pudding. The plum pudding does not contain plums but dried currants, raisins, and apples. It is not cooked as we think of pudding, but steamed in a container, getting a breadish consistency. The suet is used in place of another type of fat; its very gradual melting insures a delicate crumb.

2 c. finely chopped suet	3 c. sifted flour
2 c. seedless raisins	1 tsp. soda
1 c. chopped apple	½ tsp. salt
1 c. currants	2 Tbsp. cinnamon
1 c. light molasses	½ tsp. cloves
1 c. cold water	½ tsp. allspice

Mix the first six ingredients together and set aside. In a separate container combine the dry ingredients. Add this to the first mixture and mix well. Fill pudding molds or cans (like 1 lb. coffee cans) with tightly fitting lids, but only 2/3 full. Place molds on a trivit in a heavy kettle over, not sitting in, one inch simmering water. Cover tightly and steam for three hours. Add additional water to steaming kettle as needed so water doesn't boil away. Remove from heat, remove lids, let stand a half hour, and unmold. Serve the pudding with a lemon hard sauce or the following wine sauce.

1 c. sugar	1 well-beaten egg
1 c. butter	1/2 c. brandy
1/2 c. red wine	

Cream together sugar and butter. Add the well beaten eggs and wine. Stir over, not in, boiling water several minutes until mixture is well heated. Flame the pudding with the 1/2 c. brandy as it is brought to the table. Note: Alcohol is released from wine and brandy with heat and is not a factor in the final product.

Slowing Down

by Jerry Apps

While the winds of winter pour over the land, much of nature slows down, relaxes, and waits for the rejuvenation of spring. The black oaks stand naked at Roshara, except for the few dead leaves that rattle in the breeze. But new growth, new life for the oaks waits in the buds that are varnished and waterproofed. The oaks rest throughout the cold days of winter, snapping and cracking when the temperature dips below zero, gently swaying in the face of a northwest wind.

Deep within a hollow oak, a full grown queen hornet sleeps half-frozen, waiting for the warmer days of March and April. Roshara's pond, buried in waist-deep snow, carries a heavy layer of ice, keeping out the sun's rays and preventing the water plants from producing life-giving oxygen for the fish. The fish move slowly, using as little oxygen as possible, waiting until the ice melts and a new supply of oxygen mixes with the water. Along the banks of the pond, frogs sleep in hibernation, not really living but none-theless staying alive.

Much of the year is spent preparing for winter. Animals eat heavily in the fall, laying on a protective coating of fat. Squirrels bury acorns throughout the woodlot, spending the long winter days in search of their caches.

Songbirds and many kinds of waterfowl prepare for winter by flying south, leaving the problem of survival in a frigid land behind.

But people, though nature suggests that they should, seldom slow down in winter. The natural urge in winter is to take it a little easier, to sit by the fire on a cold afternoon with feet propped up on a chair and read a good book . . . or just nap. Or throw tip-ups in the back of the car and go ice fishing, and sit around a warm fire swapping tales and relaxing.

In our hurry-up world we're led to believe there is no time for slowing down in winter, no time to take it easy when the cutting winds whistle around the corner of the house.

Unlike the rest of nature, we hurry through winter cursing the snow that makes roads slippery, despising the cold that tightens auto engines. Perhaps we too should learn to slow down some in winter and enjoy the beauty of the snow and cold. Perhaps we need, more than we realize, an opportunity to retreat from the pressures of the rest of the year.

St. Joseph's Church, Madeline Island

Early Celebrations

BLACKROBES, VOYAGEURS AND NATIVE AMERICANS

La Fête de Noel

The Lord gave us for our (Christmas) supper a porcupine large as a suckling pig, also a rabbit. It was not much for eighteen persons, but the Holy Virgin and her spouse, St. Joseph, were not so well treated on this very day in Bethlehem.

Father Paul LeJeunne, c. 1665

New Year's Gifts

After coasting a hundred and eighty leagues along the Southern shore of Lake Superior,—where it had been our Lord's will often to test our patience by storms, famine, and weariness by day and night,—finally, on the first day of October, we arrived at Chagouamigong, whither our ardent desires had been so long directed.

This part of the Lake where we have halted is between two large Villages, and forms a sort of center for all the nations of these regions, because of its abundance of fish, which constitutes the chief part of the peoples' sustenance.

Here we have erected a little Chapel of bark, where my entire occupation is to receive the Algonkin and Huron Christians, and instruct them; baptize and catechize the children; admit the natives, who hasten hither from all directions, attracted by curiosity; speak to them in public and in private; disabuse them of their superstitions, combat their idolatry, make them see the truths of our Faith; and suffer no one to leave my presence without implanting in his soul some seeds of the Gospel.

God has graciously permitted me to be heard by more than ten different Nations; but I confess that it is necessary, even before daybreak, to entreat him to grant patience for the cheerful endurance of contempt, mockery, importunty, and insolence from these people.

Another occupation that I have in my little Chapel is the baptism of the sick children, whom the natives themselves bring hither, in order to obtain from me some medicine; and as I see that God restores these little innocents to health after their baptism, I am led to hope that it is his will to make them the foundation, as it were, of his Church in these regions.

I have hung up in the Chapel various Pictures, as of Hell and of the universal Judgment, which furnish me themes for instruction well adapted to my Hearers; nor do I find it difficult then to engage their attention, to make them chant the *Pater* and *Ave* in their own tongue, and to induce them to join in the prayers which I dictate to them after each lesson. All this attracts so many natives that, from morning till evening, I find myself happily constrained to give them my whole attention.

God blesses these beginnings.

The first days of the year 1666 have been spent in presenting a very acceptable new-year's gift to the little Jesus—consisting of a number of children brought to me by their mothers, through a Divine inspiration altogether extraordinary to be baptized. Thus, little by little, this Church is growing.

Father Claude Allouez 1665-66

Pax Christi

I am obliged to render an account to Your Reverence since my arrival here, after a voyage of a month amid snow and ice, which blocked our passage, and amid almost constant dangers of death.

Having been assigned by Divine Providence to continue the Mission of saint Esprit,—which Father Allouez had begun, and where he had baptized the principal men of the Nation of the Algonkin,—I arrived here on the thirteenth of September, and went to visit the natives in the Clearings, who are divided among five Villages. The Hurons, to the number of four or five hundred souls, almost all baptized, still preserve a little christianity. Some of the chief men, assembled in a council, were very glad to see me at first; but when I informed them that I did not yet know their language perfectly, and that no other Father was coming to the place,— both because they had all gone to the Iroquois; and because Father Allouez, who understood them thoroughly, had been unwilling to return to them for this Winter, because they did not take enough interest in Prayer,—they acknowledged that they were well deserving of this punishment. Since then they have spoken of the matter during the Winter, and resolved to do better, as they have declared to me.

One must not hope that he can avoid Crosses in any of our Missions; and the best means to live there contentedly is not to fear them, and to expect from God's goodness, while enjoying the small ones, to have much heavier ones. After their fashion, the natives wish for us to share their miseries with them, and suffer every imaginable hardship. They are lost sheep, that must be sought for among the thickets and woods, since for the most part they cry so loudly that one hastens to rescue them from the jaws of the Wolf,—so urgent have been their petitions to me during the Winter.

Father Jacques Marquette, 1669-70

French Airs, Canticles and the Sound of a Flute

The first concern of the father Louis Andre was to visit all the lodges to teach the children, and to apply the mysteries of our religion. The days were too short to satisfy the holy curiosity of those people. They did not allow him time to take his meals until very late, nor to perform his devotions, except in some retired place where they continued to seek him. They eagerly sought to hear the spiritual songs with French airs that he sang to the children. On the pathways and in the lodges, our mysteries were made public, were received with cheers, and were stamped on their minds by means of these canticles. He composed canticles against the superstitions and vices most opposed to Christianity. He taught these canticles to the children by the sound of a soft flute. He then went everywhere with his little native musicians, declaring war against the sorcerers, the conjurers and those with many wives. And because the natives passionately love their children and suffer everything from them, they allowed the biting reproaches made through songs from the mouths of their children.

Father Claude Dablon, 1670-71

Jesous Ahatonhia
Jesus Is Born

This Christmas canticle or carol was composed in the Huron-Algonkin language in 1642 by the French Jesuit Missionary Jean de Brebeuf. The English interpretation is by J. Middleton.

Twas in the moon of wintertime
  When all the birds had fled,
That Mighty Gitchi Manitou
  Sent angel-choirs instead;
Before their light the stars grew dim,
  and wond'ring hunters heard the hymn—
Jesus your King is born, Jesus is born,
  In excelsis gloria.

Within a lodge of broken bark
    The tender Babe was found,
A ragged robe of rabbit skin
    enwrapp'd His beauty round;
But as the hunter braves drew nigh,
    The angel song rang loud and high—
Jesus your King is born, Jesus is born,
    In excelsis gloria.

The earliest moon of wintertime
    Is not so round and fair
As was the ring of glory on
    The helpless Infant there.
The Chiefs from far before Him knelt
    With gifts of fox and beaver pelt—
Jesus your King is born, Jesus is born,
    In excelsis gloria.

O children of the forest free,
    O sons of Manitou,
The Holy Child of earth and Heav'n
    Is born to day for you.
Come kneel before the radiant Boy,
    Who brings you beauty, peace and joy—
Jesus your King is born, Jesus is born,
    In excelsis gloria.

Christmastide, Lake Michigan
by Susan Burdick Davis

I wish to travel away from Green Bay for a short time and let Mrs. Therese Fisher Baird tell you some of her own experiences. As a girl, Mrs. Baird lived at Mackinac Island and, as a woman, at Green Bay. Her descendants today are very much a part of the Green Bay community.

In these stories, Mrs. Baird is taking us to Mackinac Island. This island, of course, is not in Wisconsin, but it was the source of all the supplies that came in the early French and English days to our Northwest Country. It stood like a kindly priest to welcome, encourage, and aid all travelers who sought a livelihood within the bounds of

the great northern wilderness. The lives and customs of the people
of the island and the first dwellers in our part of the Northwest were
much the same. The story of our Wisconsin, moreover, cannot ade-
quately be told without including something of the "Fairy Isle",
which really was the third "Mackinaw."

"I was particularly fond of the Island of Mackinac in winter
with its ice-bound shore. In some seasons ice mountains loomed up
in every direction, picturesque and fascinating in color. At other
seasons the ice would be as smooth as one could wish. There was
hardly any communication in winter with the outer world; for about
eight months the island lay dormant. Once a month, disturbing the
peace of the inhabitants, the mail would come across from the main-
land. Its arrival was a matter of profound and agitating interest.

"Mackinac, or Michilimackinac, (the name used when there
was more time in the world than there is today—it means 'great
turtle') was the fur trade center of the West. All the traders came
here to sell their furs and buy their supplies and the goods that they
afterwards bartered for furs in distant forests. These goods were
brought to Mackinac from Montreal in birch-bark canoes, the
Indians carrying the loads over the portages.

"The dwellers on the island were mostly Roman Catholics.
At this early day, however, there was no priest stationed here. Occasionally one would come to keep alive the little spark kindled so
long ago by the devoted Jesuit missionaries.

"Since the Catholic faith prevailed, it followed as a matter of
course that the special holidays of the church were always observed.
They were celebrated in one's own home, often with some friends
and neighbors participating. Some weeks' before Christmas, for
instance, the dwellers on the island met in turn at each other's homes
and read prayers, chanted psalms, and unfailingly repeated the
litany of the Saints. On Christmas Eve both sexes would read and
sing, the service lasting until midnight. After this a midnight treat
would be partaken of by all.

"The last meeting of this sort that I attended on the island was
at our own home in 1823. This affair was considered the occasion
for the high feast of the season, and no pains were spared to make
the meal as good as the island afforded. The cooking was done at
an open fire. I wish that I could recall the bill of fare in full. We will
begin with the roast pig; then followed roast goose, chicken pie,

and round of beef a la mode; pattes d'ours—bear's paws, so-called from their shape, and made of chopped meat baked in a crust; sausage; head-cheese; souse; small fruit preserves; many small cakes. Such was the array. No one was expected to partake of each dish, unless he so chose.

"Christmas, itself, was observed as a holy-day. The children were kept at home and from play until nearly night-time, when they were permitted to run out and bid their friends a 'Merry Christmas'. The evening was spent at home, however, as I have suggested.

As soon as la fête de Noel, or Christmas-tide, had passed, all the young people were set to work to prepare for New Year's. Christmas was not the day set to give or to receive presents; this was reserved for New Year's. On the eve of that day great preparations were made by a certain class of elderly men, usually fishermen, who went from house to house in grotesque dress, singing and dancing. Following this they would receive presents. Their song was often terrifying to little girls as the gift asked for in the song was la fille aînée, the eldest daughter. The song was as follows:

> Bonjour, le Maître et la Maîtresse,
>   Et tout le monde du loger;
> Si vous voulez nous rien donner, dites-le nous;
>   Nous vous demandons seulement la fille aînée.

> (Good-day to you, Master and Madam,
>   And all the people of the house;
> If you wish to give us nothing, tell us so;
>   All we ask is the eldest daughter.)

As these grotesque visitors were always expected, every one was prepared to receive them. Their visit ended the last day of the year. After they were gone the family gathered in evening prayer, and the children retired early. At the dawn of the New Year each child would go to the bedside of his parents to receive their benediction—a most beautiful custom.

The Wooden Shoe of Little Wolff
A French Christmas Tale
by François Coppée

Once upon a time, very long ago, there was a little boy named Wolff. He was seven years old, and because he was an orphan he was taken care of by an aunt. She was a hard and selfish old woman who breathed a sigh of regret every time she gave her nephew a bowl of soup.

But little Wolff was naturally so good that he loved the old woman just the same, although she frightened him very much. He could never look at her without trembling, for fear she would scold him.

Wolff's aunt was known through all the village to have a stocking full of money in the house, but she made Wolff wear very old and ragged clothes. The schoolmaster, who liked best those pupils who were well dressed, was very unkind to Wolff and often punished him unjustly. The other pupils, too, made fun of Wolff's ill-fitting clothes. The poor little fellow, therefore, was as miserable as the stones in the street, and when Christmas came hid himself in out-of-the-way corners to cry.

The night before Christmas the schoolmaster was to take all of his pupils to midnight mass. As it was a severely cold winter, the boys set out for church warmly wrapped and bundled up, with fur caps pulled over their ears, heavy jackets, woolen mittens, and thick, heavy-nailed boots with strong soles. Only little Wolff came shivering in the clothes that he wore weekdays and Sundays, and with nothing on his feet but coarse socks and heavy wooden shoes. Wood is not warm at all, but cold.

His thoughtless comrades made a thousand jests about his rough dress; but little Wolff was so occupied in trying to keep warm that he took no notice of them.

The troop of boys, with their master at their head, started for the church. They boasted of the fine suppers that were awaiting them at home. They spoke, too, of what the Christ Child would bring them, and of how they would be very careful to leave their wooden shoes near the chimney before going to bed. For in France at that time the children put out their wooden shoes instead of hanging up their stockings. The eyes of those boys sparkled, as they saw in imagination pink paper bags filled with burnt almonds, toy soldiers drawn up in battalions in their boxes, menageries of toy animals, and amusing jumping jacks.

Little Wolff knew from experience that his stingy old aunt would send him to bed without his supper, but, remembering how all the year he had been good and industrious, he hoped that the Christ Child would not forget him. So he, too, looked forward to putting his wooden shoes in the ashes of the fireplace.

When the midnight mass was concluded, everyone rose and left the church, Now, under the porch, sitting on a stone seat, a child was sleeping. He was clad in a robe of white linen, but his feet were bare in spite of the cold. He was not a beggar, for his robe was new and clean, and near him on the ground were some tools which a carpenter's apprentice might carry. Under the light of the stars, his face bore an expression of divine sweetness, and his long locks of golden hair seemed to form a halo about his head. But the child's feet, blue in the cold of that December night, were sad so see.

The boys who were so well clothed and shod for the winter passed heedlessly by the unknown child. One of them, a wealthy lad, even looked at the waif with scorn.

But little Wolff, the last to come out of the church, stopped, full of compassion, before the beautiful sleeping child.

"Alas!" said the orphan to himself, "it is too bad this poor boy has to go barefoot in such cold weather. But what is worse, he has not even a shoe to set out while he sleeps tonight, so that the Christ Child can put something there to comfort him in his misery."

So, out of the goodness of his heart, little Wolff took the wooden shoe from his right foot, and laid it in front of the sleeping child. Then, limping along with only one shoe and dragging his shoeless sock through the snow, he went home.

"Look at that worthless fellow!" cried his aunt. "What have you done with your wooden shoe, you little wretch?"

Little Wolff did not know how to deceive. Although he was shaking with terror, he tried to stammer out some account of the good deed he had done.

But the old woman laughed scornfully.

"Ah, this young man thinks he is rich enough to give away his wooden shoe to beggars! That is something new! Well, since you are so generous, I am going to put the remaining shoe in the chimney, and I promise you the Christ Child will leave something there to whip you with in the morning. And you shall pass the day tomorrow on dry bread and water. We shall see if you give away your shoe next time to the first vagabond that comes along."

So the wicked woman, after giving the poor boy a good spanking, made him climb up to his bed in the attic. Grieved to the heart, the child went to bed in the dark, and soon fell asleep, his pillow wet with tears.

But the next morning, when the old woman went downstairs, what a wonderful sight met her eyes! She saw the great chimney full of beautiful playthings, and sacks of delicious candies, and all sorts of good things. And there, to her surprise she saw the right shoe—the one that her nephew had given to the little waif, standing by the side of the left shoe which she herself had put there.

"Goodness gracious!" the aunt exclaimed in unbelief.

Little Wolff, hearing his aunt's exclamation, ran downstairs and stood in ecstasy before all these splendid presents.

Suddenly there were loud peals of laughter out-of-doors. The old woman and the little boy hurried outside, where all the neighbors were gathered around the public fountain. What had happened? Oh, something very amusing and very extraordinary! The children of all the rich people of the village, those whose parents had wished to surprise them with the most beautiful gifts, had found only sticks in their shoes.

Then the orphan and the old woman, thinking of all the beautiful things that were in their chimney, were full of amazement. Presently they saw the priest coming toward them, wonderingly. In the church porch, where a child, clad in a white robe and with bare feet, had rested his sleeping head the evening before, the priest had just found a circle of gold incrusted with precious stones.

The people realized then that the beautiful sleeping child, with the carpenter's tools beside him, was the Christ Child in person, become for an hour such as he was when he had worked in his parents' house. And they bowed their heads before the miracle that the good God had seen fit to work, to reward the faith and charity of little Wolff.

* * * * *

Worship is in the heart
and if the true God is not the God of your heart . . .
You render not to him that glory
which is his due . . .

Samuel Mazzuchelli, O.P. December 25, 1831

Frontier Festival
by Albert G. Ellis

A recollection of how Christmas Day was observed at Fort Howard in Green Bay under the command of United States Army Colonel John McNeil.

The Colonel, an Eastern Yankee, learned that French people at the Bay celebrated Christmas as a high festival, so he decided to help his men and the citizenry honor the day in these "ends of the earth."

He sent formal invitations for dinner and a ball to everyone. Food was prepared for one hundred guests, and on December 25, 1823, a big hall at the fort was filled with French, Indians, and Americans sharing holiday greetings.

Clothing ran from the latest Parisian styles to buckskin coats, pants, petticoats, and moccasins.

None of the elite considered himself over-dressed nor none of the citizens . . . reproached himself with the least want of etiquette, or of intended disrespect to their host, on account of costume or manner.

The dinner equalled one expected in a more civilized setting in quantity if not in kind. Venison, bear meat, porcupine, geese, ducks, and many fish headed by that kind of all the fish tribe, the sturgeon, were offered for the main course. Dinner, dancing, and revelry lasted . . . throughout Christmas night.

Thus did this big-hearted man of war delight to transform this outpost of the Western wild, hitherto in its winters especially a place of desolation, solitude, ennui, and almost despair, to one of unalloyed happiness, animated life, and real pleasure.

Feasting and Native American Food

*Of foods associated with holiday feasts many, such as wild rice, squash, cran-
berries, cherries, turkey and geese have historically been found in Wisconsin.
The following accounts are descriptions of Native American food by early
visitors to the state.*

Wild Rice

As a reward for passing this way, rough and dangerous, we
enter into the most beautiful country ever seen—prairies on all
sides, as far as the eye can reach, separated by this river [upper Fox],
flowing gently through them. We see small hills with groves of
trees here and there, as if planted to shade the traveler from the
ardent heat of the sun. To paddle on this river is to repose oneself.

Here are elms, oaks and similar trees, but none with bark suited
to cover cabins or make canoes. For this reason, these natives do not
go on the water, and they have houses made of rushes bound together
in mats. Grape vines, plum trees and apple trees are seen in passing,
and invite the traveler to stop and taste their fruits, which are very
sweet and abundant. All the borders of this river, flowing tranquilly
through the prairies, are thick with wild rice, of which the birds are
wonderfully fond. Game is so abundant that we kill it without stopping. With such diversions, one does not tire of floating on these
lakes and rivers.

This country is all prairie for many leagues around. Among
these rich pastures are found buffalo, which the natives call *pisikiou*.
The natives use buffalo hides as robes and fur linings to protect
themselves against the cold. The buffalo's flesh is delicious. Its fat
mixed with wild rice makes the most delicate dish in this country.

Father Claude Dablon, 1671

* * * * *

I put our voyage under the protection of the Blessed Virgin
Immaculate, promising her that if she did us the grace to discover
the great river, I would give it the name "Conception." With these
precautions, we made our paddles play merrily over the Lake of the
Illinois [Lake Michigan].

The first nation we met was the Folles Avoine [Menominee], and I entered their river [Menominee River]. The wild rice, from which they take their name, is a kind of grass which grows spontaneously in little rivers with muddy bottoms, and in marshy places. it rises above the water in June, and keeps rising until September. natives then go in canoes across the fields of wild rice, and shake the ears on their right and left into the canoe as they advance.

Father Jacques Marquette, 1673

＊　＊　＊　＊　＊

Having received a request for some of this native grain to send abroad, and knowing that the smoked rice, such as the Indians usually bring in, will not germinate, I this day dispatched my interpreter in a canoe, with some Indians, to the northern shores of the straits to gather some of it for seed; the result was successful. This plant may be deemed a precious gift of nature to the natives, who spread over many degrees of northern latitude. They call it *mon-o-min*.

Henry Schoolcraft, 1822

Wild Rice Dressing

1 c. wild rice	1 c. chopped celery
1 c. brown rice	1/2 c. sauteed mushrooms or
1 tsp. salt	1 - 4 oz. can, drained
giblets from fowl	1 tsp. dried rosemary
2 Tbsp. butter	1/2 c. chopped almonds
1/2 c. chopped onion	

Chop giblets. Place in 7 cups water, bring to boil, and simmer for about 15 minutes. Remove giblets (this is to add flavor to rice; if you plan to use this as a side dish do not let lack of giblets discourage you. Omit this step). Stir in rice, bring to rolling boil and cover, simmering for 45-55 minutes until liquid is absorbed and rice is puffy. Meanwhile saute chopped onion and celery in butter. Add onions, celery, mushrooms, rosemary and almonds to rice mixture. Use as a stuffing for fowl or as sidedish. Yield: 5 cups.

Cranberries

When I was small the Winnebago generally went to pick cranberries after they were through taking care of their gardens. We used to do that too. When we arrived at the marsh there were many Indians who camped together there and picked cranberries. The men used rakes and the women picked by hand. As the women were picking and they reached the edge of the ditch, they all sat on the edge of the ditch in a long row, side by side. They picked ahead of themselves in a straight line, a bushel-sized box at each woman's side. They would put aside as many boxes as they thought they would fill so they would not run out of boxes. They left their boxes as they filled them, and if you looked down a line you could see the row of filled boxes. As they filled each box they took along another empty box. At noon they went back to the camp to eat. Some people even brought their lunches along and ate there at the marsh. I used to think it was great fun when we took food and ate outside.

That cranberry picking place is gone now. Iron Mountain Marsh they used to call it and I do not even know the English name for it. That cranberry marsh no longer exists because at one time a big forest fire came through there. When the people fled they said that they had to put the old people in the ditches. They could not flee with them in time so they put the old people in the water in the ditches. I believe the marsh ceased to exist at that time. The entire stand of cranberry bushes was burned up.

Mountain Wolf Woman, *Audiobiography of a Winnebago Indian Woman*

* * * * *

They grow in swamps, and are ripe in October. I was told that half the Indian families then absent from the village had gone "dans les ottakas," or to the cranberry harvest. All the American settlers preserve large guantities of this pleasant bitter-sweet and refreshing berry. It has recently become a valuable article of export, and one of the settlers boasted that he exported several tons annually. The poor Indians have to do the principal work: they go off with squaw and children into the swamp, often forty miles away, build a temporary shelter there, and pick as many berries as they can. The "great preservers" then buy their harvest of them. Although the berries are ripe in October, it is always better to pluck them later in winter. The fruit has, namely, the peculiarity that it does not fall off of itself; it remains on the branch, and will go on ripening even beneath the snow. The old berries may be seen still on the bush when the new leaves and blossom are already put forth. These ottakas do not require drying or preserving, for they keep through the whole winter in the Indian lodges, and are for a long time as fresh as if just plucked from the tree.

Johann Kohl, *Kitchi-Gami*

* * * * *

Most accounts date the first commercial use of cranberries in Wisconsin to January, 1829, when Ebenezer Childs took eight "loads" of them (probably picked by Menominee Indians) from Green Bay to Galena, Illinois, trading them for provisions to feed shingle makers who were at work in the unsettled regions along the Wisconsin River in Juneau County. Indians—along with settlers in the following decades—descended on the marshes in September and October each year to harvest the crop, bartering or selling most of it in an expanding market. Beginning in 1849, the *Milwaukee Sentinel* gave almost annual reports on the state of the cranberry crop, though domestication of it was more than a decade off.

Settlers in the Berlin area, especially in the town of Aurora in Waushara County, were among the first to buy cranberry bogs. Some, like James and Dick Carey in about 1850, fenced their best bogs to prevent unauthorized picking.

Harva Hacten, *The Flavor of Wisconsin*

* * * * *

The owner of a cranberry marsh has a better thing today, than an oil well or a gold mine, because his 'mine' grows better the more it is worked."

Berlin *Courant*, 1866

Cranberry Relish

2 c. sugar
2 c. water
4 c. cranberries, raw
2 Tbsp. grated orange rind

Please sugar and water in saucepan. Stir until sugar is dissolved and boil stirring occasionally for about 5 minutes. Then add cranberries; simmer another 5 minutes with pan uncovered. Add orange rind, then pour into a large mold which has been rinsed in cold water. Chil until firm. Unmold to serve.

Cranberry Muffins

1 3/4 c. flour
1/2 c. oat bran
3/4 tsp. salt
1/3 c. sugar
3 tsp. baking powder

2 eggs
1/4 c. vegetable oil
1 c. milk
1 c. chopped cranberries
1 c. chopped nuts
1 tsp. grated orange rind

Mix first five ingredients in a bowl. Set aside. Beat eggs, oil, and milk. Add liquids to dry ingredients in a few swift strokes. Batter may be lumpy. Fold in cranberries and nuts and orange rind. Bake at once in a preheated 400° oven for about 20 minutes.

* * * * *

The natives used to consider cranberry gathering one of their regular harvests, and an unusually prolific season a god-send; but the never-satiated progress of the settlers has steadily encroached upon their domain, until the once powerful tribe of Menominees will have to seek the headwaters of the Wisconsin . . . to find a scant supply of the delicious fruit that they were wont to gather in such profusion. . . .

Berlin *Courant*, 1861

Cherries

Near the borders of the lake grow a great number of sand cherries, which are not the less remarkable for their manner of growth, than for their exquisite flavor. They grow upon a small shrub, not more than four feet high, the boughs of which are so loaded that they lie in clusters on the sand. As they grow only on the sand, the warmth of which probably contributes to bring them to such perfection, they are called sand cherries. The size of them does not exceed that of a small musket ball, but they are reckoned superior to any other sort for the purpose of steeping in spirits.

Jonathan Carver, *Journals*, 1766

* * * * *

Like the wild plum, the wild cherry is very common in this country. It is found extensively on the edge of the smaller prairies in the forest, where hay is made. The cherries, which are ripe in August, are called by the English "sand cherry," and by the Canadians "la cerise a grappe." The women collect them and prepare them in various ways. One mode is smashing the cherries between two flat stones, then mixing them with the fat of roebuck or other animals, and boiling the whole till it forms a dough. It is then cached in makaks. In winter, when they wish to do a guest honour, and other fresh things are wanting, they will produce this. "C'est tres bon!"

J. Kohl, *Kitchi Gami*

For the last hundred years Door County has been recognized as a top producer of tart cooking cherries. Like Jonathan Carver and Johann Kohl growers found the soil favorable for cultivation of a plant that became an industry. The following recipe can be quickly made and served whenever honored guests turn up unexpectedly—as can happen at holiday time—and served 'when other fresh things are wanting. "C'est très bon!"'

Christmas Cherry Crunch

3/4 c. cherry juice	1 1/2 c. oatmeal
2 1/2 Tbsp. tapioca	1/2 tsp. baking powder
3/4 c. butter or margarine	1/2 tsp. baking soda
1 1/2 c. packed brown sugar	1/2 tsp. salt
1 1/2 c. flour	3 c. drained canned red cherries

Mix cherry juice with tapioca and let stand for 15 minutes. Meanwhile melt butter in a large pan and mix sugar, flour, oats and other dry ingredients together with butter. Put half of this mixture in a 9" x 13" pan. Evenly pour drained cherries over flour mixture, then add juice mixture. Sprinkle remaining dry ingredients over fruit. Bake 30 to 35 minutes at 350° oven until brown. Serve warm, topping with whipped cream or vanilla ice cream. Canned pie filling may be substituted.

* * * * *

May the fire
of this log
warm the cold;
may the hungry
be fed; may the
weary find rest,
and may all enjoy
Heaven's peace.

Traditional Prayer for the lighting of the Yule Log

The Prospect of
Winter on a Frontier Outpost

by Henry Schoolcraft

Henry Schoolcraft explored the origins of the Mississippi and the Western Reaches of the Louisiana Territory, as reported in his Narratives, 1818-1819. *He was appointed Indian agent for the Lake Superior region by President Monroe in 1822. His chief aim was scholarly as he undertook to study the Indian languages and write a grammar and dictionary. Here he recalls his first Wisconsin winter on the outpost of the frontier.*

Philosophers may write, and poets may sing of the charms of solitude, but when the experiment comes to be tried, on a practical scale, such as we are now, one and all, about to realize, theories and fancies sink wonderfully in the scale. For some weeks past, everything with the power of motion or locomotion has been exerting itself to quit the place and the region, and lie to more kindly latitudes for the winter. Nature has also become imperceptibly sour tempered, and shows her teeth in ice and snows. *Man-kind* and *bird-kind* have concurred in the effort to go. We have witnessed the long-drawn flight of swans, brant, and cranes, towards the south. Singing birds have long since gone. Ducks, all but a very few, have also silently disappeared, and have probably gone to pick up spicy roots in the Susquehannah or Altamahs.

Prescient in the changes of the season, they have been the first to go. Men, who can endure greater changes and vicissitudes than all the animal creation put together, have lingered longer; but at last one after another has left Pa-wa-teeg, till all who *can* go have gone. Col. Brady did not leave his command till after the snow fell, and he saw them tolerably "cantoned." The last vessel for the season has departed—the last mail has been sent. Our population has been thinned off by the departure of every temporary dweller, and lingering trader, and belated visitor, till no one is left but the doomed and fated number whose duty is here, who came here to abide the winter in all its regions, and who cannot, on any fair principle or excuse, get away. They, and they alone, are left to winter here. Of this number I am a resigned and willing unit, and I have endeavored to prepare for the intellectual exigencies of it, by a systematic study and analysis of the Indian language, customs, and history, and character. The amusements of a winter, in the latitude, are said to be rather novel, with their dog trains and creole sleighs. There are some noble fellows of the old "North West" order in the vicinity. There are thus the elements, at least, of study, society, and amusement. Whatever else betide, I have good health, and good spirits, and bright hopes, and I feel very much in the humor of enjoying the wildest kind of tempests which Providence may send to howl around my dwelling.

Sharing Their Bounty
by Johan Kohl

An educated American told me a circumstance, proving, in a most affecting manner, how capable the Indians are of liberal charity, even in their own poverty. About twenty years back, he said that he was travelling in the savage north of Wisconsin. He and his two comrades had expended all their provisions. It was winter, and deep snow covered forest and plain, so that they found difficulty in advancing, and could not possibly kill any game. They marched on for three days without sustenance, and were in a state of deep distress. At length, to their delight, they discovered an Indian lodge, entered it, and begged some food. Unfortunately, the Indians had nothing to offer, and replied to their guests' complaints with others even worse: "We," they said, "have been fasting nearly so many weeks as you have days. The deep snow has prevented us killing anything. Our two sons have gone out to day, but they will return as usual, with empty hands. Other Indians, however, live twenty miles to the north, and it is possible they are better provided than we are."

The American and his comrades, tortured by hunger, set out at once on snow-shoes to try their luck with their neighbors; but they had scarce gone four or five miles, when they heard a yell behind them, and saw an Indian hurrying after them on snow-shoes. "Hi! halloh! you men, stop! Come back!"—"What's the matter?"— "Our lads have returned. They have shot a deer, and brought it home. We have now a supply, and I have hastened to tell you of it." The European travellers turned back, and were stuffed with food, though the deer was small and the family large.

I have, I confess, never seen any starving Indians reduced to extremities, but all the Voyageurs here present have experienced it, for the satisfaction of hunger is here the standing question the year through. They are almost always in a state of want. All the Voyageurs I questioned were unanimous in their verdict that the Indians, even when starving, never lose their desire to share, but do not easily give up their courage, hope, and so to speak, their confidence in God.

Christmas on the Range
by Daniel Berrigan

There was a Christmas ritual.

A skinny tree, a few lights and trinkets, a gift or two. To the boy, what a miracle!

On that morning a great to-do arose surrounding small matters. Dining plates had been set out the night before, around the living-room table, a name beside each place. Sometime during the night, the mother, helped by one of the older boys, placed on each plate, meagerly or generously, depending on the current state of the exchequer, the following items: a handful or two of hard candy, three or four chocolates, an orange. Beside, a toy or an article of new clothing.

A clamor arose on Christmas morning at sight of such wonders! (No containing oneself; nor, indeed, any effort worth speaking of to contain us.) Our own portion, slice, the edible, delightful world! The boy enchanted, astray in his wits; why, the world itself was made of rock candy! See, a morsel of that world falls to his hands!

The round plate from which he has eaten, day after dull day, his dull portion; now a few trifles are heaped on it; colors, smells, the very marrow of happiness!

The world cheats, ever-larger portions, stakes, enterprises, Pyrrhic conquests. Other Christmases, better gifts, we weigh what lies in our hands; our eyes take on the narrowed meanness of those who know a pennyweight of gold from a pound of feathers. And all is lost.

Daniel Berrigan is a well-known latter-day blackrobe from the Lake Superior Iron Range town of Winton, Minnesota.

Santa's Show
Thomas Nast, 1890

Just Before Christmas

The Christmas Program

by Dolores Curran

For one magic evening each year, our one-room schoolhouse in southern Wisconsin was turned into a theater. The December night might be snowy and cold, but inside our snug schoolroom the furnace roared, pine branches scented the air, and the soft glow of Christmas lights fell on the proud faces of parents, neighbors, and friends. On makeshift benches entire families crowded together, waiting excitedly for the moment when a small hand would part the burlap curtains on the sawhorse-and-plank stage and a small voice would announce, "Uh ... welcome ... uh ... to our Christmas program and here's 'Silent Night'."

Perhaps the opening song wasn't appropriate to the evening's entertainment ahead, but our audience was too busy looking forward to the pieces (poems) and dialogs (skits) to let that bother them.

To the country kids of yesterday, the Christmas program was the social event of the year, with the county fair and the school picnic running very distant second and third. Our big fear, of course, was the chance we'd get sick and be unable to take part in the program, and from the first of December on, we carefully denied having any headaches, stomach-aches, or sore throats. Many's the child who, like a martyr, concealed illness for a week, only to collapse in the car on the way home. But it was contented collapse—after the program.

43

On the big day, the schoolroom was gayly decorated. We were dismissed an hour early, the only day of the year this was permitted, and our fathers came to stack the desks in the hall and set up sawhorses and plank benches in the temporary theater. A freshly cut pine was trimmed, and an extra supply of coal and logs for the furnace was brought in.

At home, tension had been running high the last few days before the program. Our teacher had enjoined us to rehearse at home until our parents were sick of us. My sister, an accomplished pianist for her age, was always relentless in practicing her Christmas selection, and I can recall overhearing my dad asking my mother, "Haven't we had enough of that d.. song?" So familiar with the parts of the young actors did the families become that it wasn't at all unusual to have a parent coach a faltering child from the audience, or a preschooler recite the lines along with an older brother or sister.

My mother started getting us dressed shortly after the cows were milked, and once each of us was dressed, we sat, without moving, for fear of getting mussed. The boys were packed into white shirts, whose sleeves were usually too short, and bow ties, which were always slanted. Then a liberal quantity of hair oil was applied. For the girls it was sheer heaven. We were able to abandon for one evening those horrible, itchy, long, brown, ribbed, cotton stockings—our town must have been the only place in the country where they were still worn. Instead, we wore knee socks, Christmas dresses, and big striped or polka dot hair bows atop our Shirley Temple curls.

Whole families attended the program together. No one even considered getting a baby-sitter, so when the curtain opened on any dialog or song, the toddlers in the audience added to the confusion by calling out "Hi, Jerry," or "Mamma, there's Ellen!" Generally, the person being singled out blushed and refused to acknowledge the recognition, which just encouraged the younger brother or sister to shout a little louder.

Each program consisted of several dialogs by the older kids and a piece by each of the younger ones. Since our school budget was slim, we used dialog and piece books like *That Good Christmas Book* and *Spicy Dialogs and Plays* over and over, so that anyone in the community who had seen his third program had sampled all the dramatic offerings available.

The biggest boy in school acted as emcee and some of them were pretty good. I remember one who couldn't find the opening in the curtain to get back on the stage. He finally turned to the audience, shrugged his shoulders, and said, "I guess it healed."

Actually, the evening's worst hurdle came first. Every year the youngest boy—and some were pretty young because we could start first grade at four—recited the piece by Eugene Field titled "Jest 'Fore Christmas." It started like this,

> *Father calls me William,*
> *Sister calls me Will,*
> *Mother calls me Willie,*
> *But the fellers call me Bill,*

and ended like this,

> *'Most all the time, the whole year round,*
> *There ain't no flies on me,*
> *But jest 'fore Christmas,*
> *I'm as good as I kin be!*

The whole school rooted for this youngster because if anyone could ruin the program, he could. Many a family suffered the embarrassment of having their Willie stare in stony-eyed terror at the friendly audience a short six feet in front of him and finally break into tears. At best, Willie stared at a spot on the floor or ceiling, rattled off a roll of syllables ending with "butjesforechrismasimasgoodasicanbe," and disappeared before the applause even began. Every—one—students, teacher, and audience—relaxed when this annual obstacle was overcome, and the program could proceed.

Everyone strived to do his best, because past *faux pas* on stage were rehashed each Christmas by the players and the community. One year I humiliated the family by being ultradramatic and inserting a wrong word. My line, supposed to have been "I hate men—they're all bad," came out "I hate men—they're all bare." This was near pornography when I was a schoolgirl, and they were still discussing it years later when Stevens School passed into oblivion. As colossal as my blunder was, however, I earned every starring female role for the next three years. I had to. I was the only girl above the fourth grade level, so I always played the mother or wife, and if the dialog had two adult women, my contemporary was often a foot shorter then I.

After the hour-long program of dialogs, pieces, and carols, came the real highlight of the evening. While the entire cast and audience sang, a portly farmer was stuffing himself into the district-owned Santa suit. His cue was the song, "Up on the Housetop," and if he missed it, or had beard trouble, we just sang the song over and over until he finally appeared.

Our favorite Santa was Harry Lanksford because he made the most noise and said something funny to each of us, which we cherished the whole year. Harry would sail into the steamy noisy room shouting "Ho-Ho-Ho" at the top of his voice and would startle the sleeping babies and toddlers so they buried their heads in their mothers' laps. Harry would stop at each child, tweak his nose or pull his hair, and say, "I heard your marks weren't very good lately," or "How come you're so slow at chores?" Although he said the same things every year, the audience laughed heartily while the recipient's ears burned. Harry would even stop by some of the men and say things about something they'd done. I remember he asked my dad if he'd dumped any tractors in the pond lately. Dad just laughed with the others, but I could tell he didn't like recalling it at all.

Then Harry got down to the important business of passing out the presents. Early in December we had all drawn the name of a schoolmate for whom we would purchase a Christmas gift. Several days of deep deliberation followed as we tried to find just the right thing for the person we had chosen—within our twenty-five-cent limit. The night of the program the packages were piled beneath the tree along with the presents from our teacher. She always gave something special, not useful. It might be a pretty pin or bracelet for the girls, or a bottle of perfume. For the boys, she chose a real fountain pen, a yo-yo, or something similar.

By the time the presents had been bestowed, the high excitement had spent itself and it was all over for another year. Fathers went out into the frosty air to wait for their families and to talk about new stock and machinery. Mothers tucked sleeping babies into buntings and gathered their tired stage stars together for the cold trip home. Santa disappeared behind the burlap curtains and out came Harry Lanksford, but no one really noticed.

None of us wanted to look back at the room now—the curtains on the stage looked like pieces of burlap, the theater seats looked like planks, and the tree without its bright load of presents looked very sad indeed. But the next day we went over the program in detail, criticizing and crediting, always ending up convinced that next year we'd have the best Christmas program in the county. And to us, we always did.

Jest 'Fore Christmas
by Eugene Field

Father calls me William, sister calls me Will,
Mother calls me Willie, but the fellers call me Bill!
Mighty glad I ain't a girl—ruther be a boy,
Without them sashes, curls, an' things that's worn by Fauntleroy!
Love to chawnk green apples an' go swimmin' in the lake—
Hate to take the castor-ile they give for belly-ache!
'Most all the time, the whole year round, there ain't no flies on
    me,
But jest 'fore Christmas I'm good as I kin be!

Got a yeller dog named Sport, sick him on the cat;
First thing she knows she doesn't know where she is at!
Got a clipper sled, an' when us kids goes out to slide,
'Long comes the grocery cart, an' we all hook a ride!
But sometimes when the grocery man is worried an' cross,
He reaches at us with his whip, an' larrups up his hoss,
An' then I laff an' holler, "Oh, ye never teched *me*!"
But jest 'fore Christmas I'm good as I kin be!

Gran'ma says she hopes that when I git to be a man,
I'll be a missionarer like her oldest brother, Dan,
As was et up by the cannibuls that lives in Ceylon's Isle,
Where every prospeck pleases, an' only man is vile!
But gran'ma she has never been to see a Wild West show,
Nor read the Life of Daniel Boone, or else I guess she'd know
That Buff'lo Bill and cow-boys is good enough for me!
Except' jest 'fore Christmas, when I'm good as I kin be!

And when old Sport he hangs around, so solemn-like an' still,
His eyes they keep a-sayin': "What's the matter, little Bill?"
The old cat sneaks down off her perch an' wonders what's be-
    come

Of them two enemies of Hern that used to make things hum!
But I am so perlite an' tend so earnestly to biz,
That mother says to father: "How improved our Willie is!"
But father, havin' been a boy hisself, suspicions me
When jest 'fore Christmas, I'm as good as I kin be!

For Christmas, with its lots an' lots of candies, cakes an' toys,
Was made, they say, for proper kids an' not for naughty boys;
So wash yer face an' bresh yer hair, an' mind yer p's and q's,
An' don't bust out yer pantaloons, an' don't wear out yer shoes;
Say "Yessum" to the ladies, an' "Yessur" to the men,
An' when they's company, don't pass yer plate for pie again;
But, thinking of the things yer'd like to see upon that tree,
Jest 'fore Christmas be as good as yer kin be!

*　*　*　*　*

My own chief conscious contribution to Christmas entertainment came when I was to recite "Ring Out, Wild Bells." On the night of nights I began about the third stanza to waver. But I liked reciting and had no mind to stop, so, depending on the recurrence of the refrain to buoy up the lines, I recall inserting words and phrases, and repetitions—regardless of what the poet wanted rung out and what rung in:

> ". . . love, hope joy, joy.
> Ring out, wild bells,
> Courage and hope and love and joy,
> The flying cloud, the frosty night,
> Ring out, ring out, ring out, wild bells,
> Ring out, wild bells, and let them die."

I had the stage, and nobody knew the difference who was rude enough to say so. The conscience of the prompter afterwards troubled her, and she apologized to my mother for losing the place. It was the first free verse ever introduced into Portage, Wisconsin.

Zona Gale, Portage

Like so many other people, we attended a little country school 1¼-miles from home. When weather was bad, our father would take us to school. Otherwise, we walked, unless we could hitch a ride with the farmers who hauled their milk to the cheese factory halfway between. In those days, there weren't any fast-moving vehicles on the road.

One of the most important events of the school year was the Christmas program. It was held in the afternoon, because the school-house didn't have lights until some years later. All of the parents and neighbors in the district would come to the program. Bed sheets were used as curtains, and all of the students took part with recitations and short plays, regardless of age or ability.

Lina Burkhardt Allmann, Plymouth

The Play's the Thing . . .
by Edna Houg

Through the eyes of hindsight the whole month of December seems to have been spent in getting ready for the school Christmas program (held the night of the last day of school before Christmas vacation) and for the Christmas program at church (held some night between Christmas and New Year's Eve). For the school-teacher much more than for the Sunday school superintendent it must have been an onerous month, for rural schoolteachers were judged, not on good teaching, but on good Christmas programs. She and she alone was responsible for planning the program, finding the appropriate songs and teaching them, selecting the recitations and playlets and plays, assigning the parts, drilling the participants, making the costumes, building the makeshift stage, decorating the schoolroom, getting and adorning the Christmas tree, arranging for the Christmas treats to be passed out to all the kids, large and small. She could and did solicit help, of course, but she alone was held accountable for any flaws or failures. There were no parent-teacher conferences or parent-teacher meetings in those days. Moreover, parents rarely visited school (we kids nigh to perished if one of them did!). Thus for the new teacher the Christmas program was the high court, the kids were the witnesses, and the audience of parents and neighbors was both judge and jury. And the verdict was either "Good program, good teacher," or "Poor program, poor teacher."

"They done real good, and Teacher don't have to be one bit ashamed. I'd say she had the best Christmas program yet."

"I sat in the front row and I couldn't hear a word them first 'n second graders said in the acrostic. Such a mumbo jumbo! Wouldn't you think the teacher would teach 'em to speak up?"

"Didn't they sing good though! And them three boys which sang 'We Three Kings!' They was perfect! 'Member how two years ago the boys that sang that song broke down laughin' and we all nearly died laughin' at 'em but the teacher nearly broke down and cried?"

For us kids the month of December was a month when most of the normal routines and restraints of public school were abolished for that all-important Christmas program. If we did not love school the other eight months, we loved it that month. Classes after the last recess were almost never held in December so that we could practice for the program. In the morning the first period in the day, morning exercise, extended through seventh- and eighth-grade arithmetic so that we could rehearse the songs.

As for the play rehearsals, they were every bit as earnest as the Theater Guild's rehearsals in New York of *Heartbreak House, Strange Interlude*, and *The Time of Your Life*. In every community there was always a John Barrymore or a Helen Hayes, and the Christmas program play was their opportunity to express what their shyness did not otherwise allow them to express. On the "night of nights" they surprised Teacher—yes, even themselves—with their uninhibited, high-flown expressiveness in voice, gesture, and facial expression. They may not have met the criteria of the dramatic, but no one could say that they were not melodramatic. Indeed, some school districts gained a reputation for having stars, and "outsiders" sometimes came to the Christmas program just to hear them recite or see them act.

Christmas at School

A delightful Christmas program marked the closing of school before the holidays and sent teachers and pupils home with a glow of the Christmas spirit. Generous sacks of candy were given to all the children of the village.

The following Christmas program was given:—

Opening Chorus — *"Christmas Bells"*

School.
Masque—*"The Lost Toys"*

Primary Dept.
Recitation—*"When The Boys Come Home"*

Viola Thieme.
Song—*"Santa's Helpers"*

Girls of Kindergarten and Primary Dept.
Pantomime—*"Silent Night"*
Solo—Marion Christianson
Violin—John Haas
Piano—Gertrude Pool
Recitation—*"Christmas Spirit"*

Oscar Mueller.
Playette—*"Mother Goose's Party"*

Children, Primary Dept.
Song—*"Christmas Over There"*

Grammar Grade Girls.
Reading—*"Jane Conquest"*

Flora Fleckinger
Lantern Drill—

Girls, Intermediate Dept.
Play—*"Christmas at Skeeter Corners"*

Grammar Dept.
Closing Song—*"Happy Christmas Tide"*

Arrival of Santa Claus.

Kohler News, 1918

We reproduce as a matter quite essential for Christmas morning as the Gold Quotations, or the "Latest from Europe," Mr. Clement C. Moore's felicitious poem describing the annual visit of St. Nicholas or "Santa Claus" as the children prefer to call the jolly, benevolent, old fellow. The little ones will all read it anew, and with it we pray them to take the Sentinel's tenderest wishes for a merry, merry Christmas.

Milwaukee Sentinel, December 25, 1866

A Visit From St. Nicholas

by Clement C. Moore

'Twas the night before Christmas, when all through the house
Not a creature was stirring, not even a mouse;
The stockings were hung by the chimney with care,
In hopes that St. Nicholas soon would be there;
The children were nestled all snug in their beds,
While visions of sugar-plums danced through their heads;
And mamma in her kerchief, and I in my cap,
Had just settled our brains for a long winter's nap.—
When out on the lawn there arose such a clatter,
I sprang from my bed to see what was the matter.
Away to the window I flew like a flash,
Tore open the shutters and threw up the sash.
The moon, on the breast of the new-fallen snow,
Gave a lustre of midday to objects below;
When what to my wondering eyes should appear,
But a miniature sleigh and eight tiny reindeer,
With a little old driver, so lively and quick
I knew in a moment it must be St. Nick.
More rapid than eagles his coursers they came,
And he whistled and shouted and called them by name:
"Now, Dasher! now, Dancer! now, Prancer and Vixen!
On, Comet! on, Cupid! on, Donder and Blitzen!
To the top of the porch, to the top of the wall!
Now, dash away, dash away, dash away all!"
As dry leaves that before the wild hurricane fly,
When they meet with an obstacle, mount to the sky,

So, up to the house-top the coursers they flew,
With a sleigh full of toys,—and St. Nicholas too.
And then in a twinkling I heard on the roof
The prancing and pawing of each little hoof,
As I drew in my head and was turning around,
Down the chimney St. Nicholas came with a bound.
He was dressed all in fur from his head to his foot,
And his clothes were all tarnished with ashes and soot;
A bundle of toys he had flung on his back,
And he looked like a peddler just opening his pack.
His eyes how they twinkled! his dimples how merry!
His cheeks were like roses, his nose like a cherry;
His droll little mouth was drawn up like a bow,
And the beard on his chin was as white as the snow.
The stump of a pipe he held tight in his teeth,
And the smoke it encircled his head like a wreath.
He had a broad face, and a little round belly
That shook, when he laughed, like a bowl full of jelly.
He was chubby and plump,—a right jolly old elf—
And I laughed when I saw him, in spite of myself.

A wink of his eye and a twist of his head
soon gave me to know I had nothing to dread.
He spoke not a word, but went straight to his work,
And filled all the stockings; then turned with a jerk,
And laying his finger aside of his nose,
And giving a nod, up the chimney he rose.
He sprang to his sleigh, to his team gave a whistle,
And away they all flew like the down of a thistle;
But I heard him exclaim, ere he drove out of sight:
"Happy Christmas to all, and to all a goodnight!"

The Night After Christmas

Anonymous

'Twas the night after Christmas, when all through the house
Every soul was abed, and as still as a mouse;
The stockings, so lately St. Nicholas's care,
Were emptied of all that was eatable there.
The Darlings had duly been tucked in their beds—
With very full stomachs, and pains in their heads.

I was dozing away in my new cotton cap,
And Nancy was rather far gone in a nap,
When out in the nurs'ry arose such a clatter,
I sprang from my sleep, crying—"What is the matter?"
I flew to each bedside—still half in a doze—
Tore open the curtains, and threw off the clothes;
While the light of the taper served clearly to show
The piteous plight of those objects below;
For what to the fond father's eyes should appear
But the little pale face of each sick little dear?
For each pet that had crammed itself full as a tick,
I knew in a moment now felt like Old Nick.

Their pulses were rapid, their breathings the same,
What their stomachs rejected I'll mention by name—
Now Turkey, now Stuffing, Plum Pudding, of course,
And Custards, and Crullers, and Cranberry sauce;
Before outraged nature, all went to the wall,
Yes—Lollypops, Flapdoodle, Dinner, and all;

Like pellets which urchins from popguns let fly,
Went figs, nuts and raisins, jam, jelly and pie.
Till each error of diet was brought to my view,
To the shame of Mamma and Santa Claus, too.

I turned from the sight, to my bedroom stepped back,
And brought out a phial marked "Pulv. Ipecac.,"
When my Nancy exclaimed—for their sufferings shocked her—
"Don't you think you had better, love, run for the Doctor?"
I ran and was scarcely back under my roof,
When I heard the sharp clatter of old Jalap's hoof.
I might say that I hardly had turned myself round,
When the Doctor came into the room with a bound.
He was covered with mud from his head to his foot,
And the suit he had on was his very worst suit;
He had hardly had time to put *that* on his back,
And he looked like a Falstaff half fuddled with sack.
His eyes, how they twinkled! Had the Doctor got merry?
His cheeks looked like *Port* and his breath smelled of *Sherry*.
He hadn't been shaved for a fortnight or so,
And the beard on his chin wasn't white as the snow.
But inspecting their tongues in despite of their teeth,
And drawing his watch from his waistcoat beneath,
He felt of each pulse, saying—"Each little belly
Must get rid"—here he laughed—"of the rest of that jelly."
I gazed on each chubby, plump, sick little elf,
And groaned when he said so, in spite of myself;
But a wink of his eye when he physicked our Fred
Soon gave me to know I had nothing to dread.
He didn't prescribe, but went straightway to work
And dosed all the rest, gave his trousers a jerk,
And, adding directions while blowing his nose,
He buttoned his coat; from his chair he arose,
Then jumped in his gig, gave old Jalap a whistle,
And Jalap dashed off as if pricked by a thistle;
But the Doctor exlaimed, ere he drove out of sight,
"They'll be well by tomorrow—good night, Jones, good night!"

Godey's Ladies Book, 1860

Rascal at Christmas

by Sterling North

This is an excerpt of a memoir of a Wisconsin boyhood during the WWI era. The author relates his adventures with a pet racoon named Rascal who helped him weather a time of family change: his mother's death, his brother's leaving to fight in the war, his sisters' departure for a grown-up life. Rascal also taught the author a respect for a wild animal's habits and habitat, so different from that of a typical pet.

The first flurry of snow came early in December, whirling a few flakes into Rascal's hollow in the tree. I feared that a real blizzard might make that den quite uncomfortable. From a piece of sheet copper I fashioned a hood over the entrance, and I lined the hole itself with old blankets and an outgrown sweater of mine so that my racoon would have a snug winter nest. Rascal took an immediate fancy to the sweater, perhaps associating it with me.

As cold weather set in, Rascal grew sleepy. Racoons do not actually hibernate, but they do sleep for many days at a time, emerging only occasionally to pad around in the snow seeking a full meal. Every morning before I left for school I would go into the cage and reach into the hole. I wanted to make sure that Rascal was safe and comfortable. It was a great satisfaction to feel his warm, furry body breathing slowly and rhythmically, and to know that he was sleeping soundly in his pleasant home.

Sometimes he stirred when I petted him, and murmured in his sleep. Now and then he awoke sufficiently to poke his little black-masked face out of the hole to look at me. I always rewarded him with a handful of pecans.

I realized, of course, that our partial separation was only temporary. Many living things sleep through the winter: my woodchucks under the barn, frogs deep in the mud, seeds in their pods, and butterflies in their cocoons. They were merely resting for spring and would awake again with a great burst of new life. Rascal and I would have wonderful times together when the warm months returned.

So with a final pat or two I would tell my pet to go on sleeping. And Rascal, drowsy-eyed, would curl into a ball and return to his winter slumbers.

With Christmas coming, I turned to the pleasant tasks of buying a tree and sweeping and decorating the house. My father paid little attention to such matters, and furthermore he was again away on business.

Almost immediately I realized that Rascal presented a new and difficult problem. It had always been our custom to invite some of the animals to be with us on Christmas Eve when we distributed the gifts. In the past we usually had limited the four-footed delegation to Wowser and the best behaved of the cats. But it was unthinkable to exclude Rascal, who, however, could never discipline his hands when shining objects were within his reach.

He could examine a glass paperweight or lift the lid of the sugar bowl without breaking glass or crockery. But I could well imagine the damage he might do to the fragile glass balls and figurines on the Christmas tree.

How could we have both Rascal and a Christmas tree? And yet we must have both. The answer to this dilemma struck me as a real inspiration.

There was a large semicircular bay extending from the living room, with six windows that overlooked the flower garden. This was where we always mounted our Christmas tree. I bought and decorated a thick spruce, which tapered gracefully to the star at its tip and nearly filled the bay with its fragrant greenery. This took me most of one Saturday. Then I made careful measurements of the rectangular opening leading to the bay and hastened to my work bench in the barn. I had sufficient chicken wire left from building the cage to cover a frame, designed carefully and precisely to fit the opening I had just measured. In less than an hour I was maneuvering this construction through the big, double front door into the living room. The lumber was white and new, the chicken wire shining. But for a few moments I hesitated before nailing it to the unmarred woodwork of our responsible old house. Still, it required but one nail at each corner of the frame, and I could fill the holes later with putty or wood-filler. Another few minutes and the job was complete. And there, safe behind the wire, was the decorated tree, every bauble secure from my raccoon.

I put a Christmas wreath above the fireplace, laced Christmas ribbons through the ribs of my canoe frame, hung a few sprigs of holly from archways and chandeliers, and stood back to admire the total effect. I was immoderately pleased with my work and could scarcely wait to show it to my father and to Jessica.

When my father returned from his trip, I led him happily into the living room and pointed to the Christmas tree, wired off from the rest of the world as though it might try to escape to its native forest.

"My word," my father said mildly. "What are you building, Sterling, another cage for Rascal?"

"You're warm," I said. "It's so that Rascal can't climb the tree and spoil the ornaments."

"Well," my father hesitated," at least it's unusual."

"Do you think Jessica will hit the ceiling?"

"She might," my father said. "You never can tell what Jessica might do."

There was one train a day from Chicago, an old ten-wheeler pulling a baggage car, a passenger coach, and sometimes a freight car and a caboose. We loved that train and listened for it to rumble across the river bridge, blow four times for the lower crossing, and come huffing and puffing up the slight grade to the station. My late grandfather had often spoken of the first train that had ever rolled over these tracks, with twenty yoke of oxen helping it up the grade. But ours was a better and much newer engine.

There seemed to be a special music to the bell of our ten-wheeler, and a special corona made by its exhaust steam as it pulled to a halt and hissed its hot vapor into the sunlight. Train time was exciting even if the passenger coach did not carry someone as much loved as my sister Jessica.

The conductor helped her down the steps and my father and I took her suitcase and her many packages. She was wearing a wide-brimmed velvet hat which looked very fashionable, a new coat with a fur collar, and high-laced shoes that came to the hem of her dress. She had recently sold several groups of poems and a short story, and she seemed quite affluent.

"Merry Christmas, Jessica. Welcome home," we cried.

She kissed us, and then held me off and looked at me critically. "You've outgrown your Mackinaw, Sterling. And you'll catch your death of cold not wearing a cap."

"He never wears a cap," my father explained.

Obviously I was clean, and had combed my stubborn curls into some semblance of order, so Jessica wasn't altogether disapproving.

We went homeward through the iron-cold air and bright sunlight, up Fulton Street, past all the stores. We turned right on Albion, past the Carnegie Public Library and the Methodist Church, then left on Rollin Street, and there we were, still laughing and chattering and asking a hundred questions in the manner of most families gathering for Christmas.

Perhaps we were extra gay to cover an underlying sadness. Mother would not be at the gracious double door to greet us. Herschel was still in France, but "alive and unwounded" as we kept repeating. Theo and her kind husband Norman would be spending Christmas in their own home far to the north. Already our closely knit family was dwindling and dispersing as all families eventually must. But the three of us would do the best we could to bring cheer to the old house.

As we entered the living room, I wasn't sure whether Jessica wanted to laugh or cry. I had done my best in decorating the tree and the canoe, which was supposed to hold our cargo of gifts. But suddenly I saw it through my sister's eyes—an unfinished boat, chicken wire, and dust on the furniture.

"You simply *can't* go on living like this!" she said, "You *must* hire a full-time housekeeper."

"But, Dottie," I pleaded, using her pet name, "I worked so hard on the tree and decorations, and the cage to keep Rascal out."

Then Jessica was laughing and hugging me in the crazy way she often acted (much the way I acted, too). She was, and is, the most spontaneously affectionate, thoughtful, brilliant, and unreasonable sister one could wish for. A very attractive combination, I have always maintained.

"At least we can take the canoe to the barn," Jessica said (not wishing to lose her advantage).

"But, Dottie, I can't take it to the barn. It's cold as blazes out there. I have to put on the canvas first."

"Well, put on the canvas, and we'll still have time to clean this room for Christmas."

"That sounds sensible," my father agreed.

"But you don't understand," I explained. "I had to spend all my money to build the cage, and then all the other money I could scrape together to buy Christmas presents, and . . ."

"Sterling, get to the point," Jessica said.

"So I haven't any money left for canvas, and it will cost about fifteen dollars, I think."

Jessica looked at my father severely, and he said, "Now be reasonable, Jessica. I'm a busy man. I can't know everything that's going on in Sterling's head and I didn't know he needed money for canvas."

Jessica sighed, realizing that we were both quite hopeless and greatly in need of her care. "Well, at least I can cook you some decent meals and clean up this house."

"It's perfectly clean," I protested. "I swept every single room and shook out the throw rugs and scoured the bathrooms. You don't know how hard I worked getting this place beautiful for you. And, besides, we like our own cooking, and we don't want a housekeeper. You sound like Theo."

"We're happy," my father said. "As happy as we can be since your mother died."

"Don't be sentimental," Jessica said fiercely, wiping tears from her own eyes. "You just wait until I get on an apron! And another thing, you're going to have a housekeeper whether you like it or not."

On the day before Christmas we wrapped our gifts in secrecy in various rooms of the house, camouflaging some in odd-sized packages. We arranged them according to the recipient: those for my father in the prow of the canoe, those for Jessica in the stern, and those for me amidships.

After an early dinner we brought in the animals—Rascal first, to allow him to wake up for the festivities, then Wowser, and finally the selected cats. Jessica immediately fell in love with my raccoon. And when she saw how he struggled to reach through the wire to touch the Christmas tree baubles, she forgave me for building the barricade.

The Yule log was blazing in the fireplace, shedding light on the tree and its ornaments and making the chicken wire gleam like a dew-drenched cobweb. The argosy of brightly wrapped gifts greatly intrigued my raccoon.

Animals, like children, find it difficult to wait for a gift which is almost within reach. So we always gave them their presents first. Each cat received a catnip mouse, making the old toms and tabbies as playful as kittens, and causing a certain amount of possessive growling. For Wowser, confined to his bath towel on the hearth, I had a new collar which Garth Shadwick had fashioned. But for my pampered pet, Rascal, I had only Christmas candies and pecans, being unable to think of a single other thing he might need.

In opening the family packages we proceeded in rotation. This gave us a chance to admire each object and to express gratitude. There were many thoughtfully chosen books, ties, socks, warm gloves, scarves—all appreciated.

The best gifts came last. Theo and Norman had been quite extravagant. They had sent Jessica a fur muff and my father a sheared beaver cap. To me they had given shoe ice skates, very rare in our region in those days. I eagerly awaited our next game of hockey.

My father brought forth from his pocket a small buckskin pouch and poured into his hand seven beautifully cut and polished agates. They were ringed like Rascal's tail, from golden yellow through oak-leaf brown to deep maroon. With unexpected forethought he had sent our best rough stones from Lake Superior to a gem-cutting firm in Chicago, insisting that they be returned in time for Christmas.

My father was pleased by our response. He chose three agates for Jessica and three for me. Then he did a most surprising thing. Calling for Rascal, he handed him the handsome little stone that the raccoon himself had found.

Always fascinated by shining objects, Rascal felt it carefully, sat up, holding it between his hands to examine it and smell it, then carried it to the corner where he kept his pennies and unceremoniously dropped it among his other treasures. He came back chirring cheerfully.

This might well have topped the gift-giving. But one more large package still lay amidships, "To Sterling, from Jessica." I was very curious but could not imagine what it might be. Upon removing the wrappings I found an unbelievable present—enough heavy, strong white canvas to cover my entire canoe. I was near to unwanted tears, but Jessica saved the day.

"Now perhaps we can get this canoe out of the living room," she said.

Wowser, Rascal, and the cats were soon asleep around us. My

father asked Jessica to read from the second chapter of St. Luke, as Mother had done on so many Christmas Eves.

"And it came to pass in those days, that there went out a decree from Caesar Augustus . . .

"And she brought forth her firstborn son, and wrapped him in swaddling clothes, and laid him in a manger; because there was no room for them in the inn . . .

"And there were in the same country, shepherds, abiding in the field, keeping watch over their flock by night . . .

"And, lo, the angel of the Lord came upon them . . . and they were sore afraid."

Faintly through the drifting snow came the strains of the church organ playing "Silent Night, Holy Night."

We put out all the pets except my raccoon—the cats to curl in the hay of the barn, Wowser to sleep in his double-walled doghouse on his blankets. But Rascal went to bed with me. As we dropped off to sleep I wondered if at midnight Christmas Eve raccoons speak as other animals are said to do.

Sterling North was born in 1906 in southern Wisconsin on the shores of Lake Koshkonong. He worked as a newspaperman in Chicago and New York; he wrote more than thirty biographies of famous Americans, the best-seller So Dear to My Heart, and poetry. Both his novel and Rascal: Memories of a Better Era were made into movies by Walt Disney.

The Christmas Costume
by Carol Ryrie Brink

In the beginning Hetty had planned to take a different one of the children with her every time she went to call on Aunt Molly Nightingale. There must be only two at a time, Aunt Molly had said, because Grandpa was so old and many people in the house confused him.

Every Saturday afternoon that fall of 1865 Hetty went to see Aunt Molly, yet, in spite of her early resolution, she always took the same person with her—and it was little Minnie. This was not because the other children did not want to go. Now that they had heard about the cabinet and Adelaide and Grandpa and the music box, they were all wild to go and see for themselves. But Mother would not let them plague Hetty.

"No," Mother said reasonably, "Hetty went when none of the rest of you would go. This is her affair."

The reason that Hetty took Minnie with her instead of Caddie or Clara or Tom or Warren had something to do with her own feeling of importance. At Aunt Molly's she was a tall, big girl named Henrietta.

Mother usually found something nice for her to carry to Aunt Molly's: some fresh doughnuts under a clean fringed napkin or a warm loaf of bread.

"I don't want you and Minnie to be the least bit of trouble to Mrs. Nightingale," Mother would always warn. "You must clean your feet well before you go in on her immaculate floors, and remember to be polite and not too chatty. I'm not at all sure that she likes to have you."

But Hetty was sure. It couldn't have been pretending that made Aunt Molly's eyes light up when she saw them standing in the doorway.

"Well, I declare! It's Henrietta and little Minnie! Come in, my dears, come in!"

When they had gone in by the dining-room stove to take off their wraps, Grandpa would look up from his knitting, or the nets which he made out of fishline, and smile at them and say, "Well, well! What little gels are these, Molly?"

"You remember, Papa—they're the Woodlawn girls, Henrietta and Minnie."

After they had taken off their wraps Hetty, with little Minnie holding fast to her hand, always went to the parlor door and opened it just a crack to look in.

"Good afternoon, Adelaide," Hetty said softly to the doll on the small sofa under the window, and little Minnie echoed, "Afternoon, Adelaide."

Adelaide never replied, but it was not a haughty silence; it was only the amiable silence of a princess who is under an enchantment which prevents her from using her tongue.

After they had paid their respects to Adelaide, they went back to Aunt Molly and asked her if there was anything they could do to help her. Sometimes she had errands for them to run; sometimes she let them help her cut calico squares for her patchwork, or she let them tidy her button box or hold a skein of yarn while she wound it into balls. Once they cut cookies for her with a cutter shaped like a man. When the cookies were placed in the pan, Aunt Molly gave them some currants to put on each man for eyes and buttons. Minnie laughed when the currant eyes went on crooked, and Hetty was obliged to help her put them straight. The currants sat on top of the white dough like black dots; but, after the men had been in the oven for a while, the dough puffed up all around the currants and became brown, and then they were real men with eyes and buttons.

Sometimes the two girls put on their wraps again and went with Grandpa to feed the chickens and gather the eggs. Grandpa could not climb into the loft where the hens were fond of stealing away to hide their eggs, but Hetty's sharp eyes could always find the stolen nests. And the day when Grandpa forgot that he had just finished feeding the chickens and started to do it all over again, Hetty and Minnie were there to remind him.

Then, when all the little chores were done, Aunt Molly would open the parlor door wide and let Hetty and Minnie give Adelaide her tea.

The footstool was the right size for a table with a fringed napkin for a tablecloth; and Adelaide had her own little set of dishes, white with a moss-rose pattern. Aunt Molly let the girls set the table and fetch the teapotful of milk from the springhouse, and cookies from the crock in the kitchen. When Aunt Molly did not make men she cut her cookies with a doughnut cutter, and the small rounds from the center of the cookies were always baked and kept by themselves for Adelaide's tea parties.

Hetty always tied one of the small fringed napkins around Adelaide's neck, so that no crumb or drop of milk should ever soil the beautiful silk dress.

"Aunt Molly," Hetty asked one day, "if you have had Adelaide since you were a little girl, how does it happen that her dress is in the latest fashion?"

"Why," said Aunt Molly, "that's because I make her a complete new outfit every year. It's just a custom that I started long ago and have always continued. You see, a dress gets quite dusty and untidy after a year's wear. I like a new dress myself once every year."

"So do I," said Hetty, and little Minnie echoed, "So do I."

"She wore a white India muslin when I first received her,"

related Aunt Molly, "but you may guess that it got rather soiled from a year's handling. So on the next Christmas I made her a red calico out of some pieces left from a frock of mine. I think I have all her costumes in a box in the attic. Should you like to see them?"

There was never a more unnecessary question. Of course Hetty and Minnie wanted to see them! They hung over the box of costumes as if it had contained Cinderella's ball gown or the coronation robes of Queen Victoria.

Out of the box came Aunt Molly's first attempt at dressmaking. It was a turkey red calico with tiny speckles of black, and it was made with a rather plain skirt and very full sleeves in the fashion of thirty years earlier.

"My goodness!" said Hetty. "Did you make it all yourself, Aunt Molly? And you were only about eleven then, I guess."

"Yes, but if you look you'll see that I didn't make it very well. I was in a hurry toward the last, and you see what long irregular stitches I made along the hem."

"It's better than we could do, isn't it, Minnie?"

"Yes, it is," said little Minnie.

"And every Christmas since that time," said Aunt Molly, "I've made Adelaide a costume."

"Every single Christmas?"

"I don't believe I've missed a one."

Then out of the box came Adelaide's costumes, one by one.

"What if you should ever miss a Christmas, Aunt Molly?" asked Hetty. "Wouldn't Adelaide feel dreadful?"

"Poor Adelaide!" said Minnie.

"I expect I'd feel even sadder than Adelaide," said Aunt Molly, smiling. "You see, I've made new dresses for her now for so many years it's become a part of Christmas. If I should ever forget it, or if something should happen to keep me from doing it, I expect I'd feel pretty bad."

"My! I guess you would!" said Hetty, and Minnie echoed. "My!"

At home Hetty and Minnie were never done describing the wonders of Aunt Molly's parlor, and the magical strangeness of her whole household.

It was a whole new world of experience which the two little girls brought home.

But one Saturday afternoon at the end of November when they knocked at Aunt Molly's door, they were surprised to see Dr. Nightingale open it.

He was very tall and grave, and now there was a little pucker of anxiety between his eyebrows on his forehead.

"Not today, I'm afraid, little girls," he said. "Come back some other day. We have sickness in the house."

"It isn't Aunt Molly, is it?" asked Hetty.

"No, it's the old gentleman," Dr. Nightingale said. "He's very old, and he's come down with a congestion in his lungs. We don't know yet if he'll pull through. Aunt Molly has her hands full nursing him."

The whole Woodlawn family was concerned. Even those who knew Grandpa only through Hetty's vivid descriptions of him had become fond of the rosy old gentleman who could not remember little girls' names.

Everyone was sad, but for Hetty and Minnie the sadness was something special. It was first of all a sadness for Grandpa and then for Aunt Molly, and last of all for themselves; for they were suddenly shut away from their Saturday world of enchantment.

They thought of Adelaide, sitting alone in the cold parlor, and they wondered if she would understand why there were no tea parties, why no one spoke to her.

Then, as the time kept moving on, another thought came to Hetty. The Woodlawns were going ahead with their own exciting plans for Christmas. Tom was making a little wooden cart for baby Joe; Clara was knitting Father a comforter for his neck to keep him warm on the drives to Eau Galle. Whenever you looked at Caddie she hid something under her apron or cried, "Just a minute, please! Don't come in till I tell you."

Hetty said to Minnie, "You remember about Adelaide's Christmas costume?"

"Oh, yes," said little Minnie.

"I wonder if there'll be one this year. I don't think Aunt Molly had started it before Grandpa got sick."

"Poor Adelaide!" said Minnie.

"Poor Aunt Molly, too," said Hetty. "You remember what she said? If ever she'd forget a Christmas, she said, she'd feel sadder than Adelaide."

"I know," said little Minnie.

"Minnie!" Hetty said. "What if we—Oh, Minnie, I wonder if we could!"

"Do you mean that *we* should make a costume?" asked Minnie, her eyes wide with astonishment.

"You know there was some wine-colored alpaca left from Clara's Sunday dress. If she would let us have it!"

"Clara or Caddie would help us, maybe," said Minnie.

"No," said Hetty. She was very decided upon this point. "No. We're the ones who have had all the good times with Adelaide. We must do it ourselves. Remember the red calico dress Aunt Molly made the first time? Some of the stitches were pretty uneven in that. And we would try as hard as we could."

"But how would we know the right size?"

"We must borrow one of the costumes and bring it home with us."

"But how would we get it?"

"We must go with Mother next time she goes."

They had been able to get one of Adelaide's dresses without anybody else knowing. It had almost seemed as if Adelaide's eyes had questioned them as she sat so sedately on her sofa in the cold parlor with its drawn shades. Perhaps she was wondering why there was no tea today, and why there had been no party for a long time. Was she, perhaps, beginning to dream of Christmas? Was she thinking, "Well, it will be different after I get my new costume"?

"It's going to be all right, Adelaide, I think," Hetty whispered, and little Minnie gave Adelaide a kiss.

They did not see Aunt Molly, and Hetty noticed that the many calendars and almanacs in the kitchen still read *November*. Aunt Molly had not remembered to tear off or fold back the November pages.

And now began a very trying time in the lives of Hetty and Minnie. The difficulty of cutting and sewing a costume for the first time was equaled only by the difficulty of keeping a secret. At last it seemed as if they would never be done by Christmas unless they took someone into their confidence; for the first bodice they made was too small when the seams were taken up, and the sleeves turned backwards instead of forwards as sleeves should do. And so one day they told Clara what they were trying to do.

Clara did not seem at all surprised. It was almost as if she had been waiting for them to ask her advice; and now she showed them how much larger one should cut a garment than it would appear to be when it was finished, and how the sleeves would be all right if they were only reversed. Luckily there was enough material.

Usually Clara was not one to tell things, but somehow the news of what Hetty and Minnie were doing got around the family circle. No one plagued or teased them about it. But the day before Christmas, when they were still taking turns at setting in the tiny stitches (which sometimes grew larger for very desperation), and when the end seemed very nearly in sight, Tom and Warren came in from the woods with a doll-sized Christmas tree. It was really a little beauty, of a most perfect shape, and they had risked their necks in the swampland to get it out for Adelaide. And then it seemed that Clara had baked tiny star-shaped cookies with loops of thread baked into them for hanging them upon the tiny branches, and Caddie had been carving and gilding tiny hazelnut baskets and stringing red cranberries.

Suddenly Adelaide's Christmas had become more important to the Woodlawn children than their own.

Mother knew about the preparations now, but she was quite reluctant to encourage them.

"I can't—I really can't have you bothering them," she said, "Until we know that Mrs. Nightingale's father is better."

Then, miraculously, about four o'clock in the afternoon Father came in, stamping the fresh snow from his boots in the back entryway, and he said, smiling around at all of them, "Well, I have good news for you."

"What is it, Father? What is it?"

"I just met Dr. Nightingale on the road, and he says that Grandpa's out of danger."

"He's going to get well?"

"He's going to get well! Furthermore," said Father, looking around at Hetty and Minnie with a twinkle in his eye, "it seems that he's been asking for the little girls who used to help him feed the chickens—Emily and Mildred, the doctor says he called them; but Mrs. Nightingale told him those were the little Woodlawn girls and he should let them know that they might come and see Grandpa for a very few minutes if they were nice and quiet."

Caddie and Clara and Tom and Warren all went across the snowy fields with Hetty and Minnie to help them carry the roast fowl Mother had sent and the Christmas tree with all the decorations—and the Christmas costume.

"We'll wait for you out by the barn," Clara said, "so we won't be any bother and so you'll have somebody to walk home with you after dark."

But first the older ones helped the two little girls put the tree in order and light the one candle which they had tied to the topmost branch. Even in her excitement Hetty felt sorry that Caddie and Clara and Tom and Warren were going to be left outside. Her conscience hurt her now because they had never yet seen Adelaide, nor the parlor, nor the cabinet.

Then Aunt Molly was opening the door for them, and crying out with surprise at sight of the little Christmas tree.

"No! It's never Christmas surely!"

"Yes, it is!" cried Hetty. "Merry Christmas, Aunt Molly!"

And little Minnie said, "Yes, it is, Aunt Molly!"

Aunt Molly's face had lost the white, troubled look which it had worn for the last month. Her little black eyes sparkled. She was almost beautiful.

"And you have brought us a tree!" she cried.

"The roast fowl is for Grandpa and you and Dr. Nightingale," said Hetty, "but the tree is for Adelaide."

"Adelaide?" said Aunt Molly. Suddenly her bright face clouded again. "Adelaide! Why, it's Christmas, isn't it? The first Christmas I ever forgot all about Adelaide. How very odd! I never thought I should—"

"Aunt Molly," Hetty said in an excited rush of words, "I hope you won't be angry with us, but we went ahead and did it. It isn't very good; but Minnie and me, we made the Christmas costume."

"You made the Christmas costume?" said Aunt Molly. She opened the package they held out, and looked very carefully at the wine-colored alpaca costume without saying a word.

"It isn't very good," Hetty repeated hesitantly.

"We got in kind of a hurry," Minnie said.

"What do you mean it isn't very good!" snapped Aunt Molly. "It's ever so much better than *I* did on *my* first one!"

Then Hetty saw that there was a glint of tears in Aunt Molly's eyes, and she knew that Aunt Molly had taken so long to speak because she had wanted to cry instead. It was quite strange. But when Aunt Molly kissed them, they knew that everything was all right—because she had never kissed them before, and this was a happy kiss.

The light of the Christmas candle was bright on Adelaide's china cheeks. It seemed to make her eyes dance, and the costume fitted perfectly.

"Papa," Aunt Molly said to Grandpa later when she had taken the girls to see him for a moment, "Papa, I forgot Adelaide's Christmas costume, but these little girls did not. They made her a beautiful one."

Grandpa smiled his little smile as if he knew a secret.

His voice seemed far away and strange, but he said, "Molly, take them in to the cabinet. Let them choose—let Gertrude and Emily choose whatever they like out of it, for a Christmas present from me."

"Anything, Papa?" asked Mrs. Nightingale.

"Anything they want," said Grandpa.

So in a moment they found themselves standing before the cabinet with the magical power to choose gifts for themselves from its wonderful shelves.

Hetty looked at the dressed fleas, at the pin with the Lord's Prayer engraved on the head, at the little china ballet dancer.

Then she thought, "Caddie would take the ostrich egg, Tom would want the boat in the bottle, Warren would want the petrified wood."

Doubtfully she looked at Minnie.

"What do you want, Minnie?"

"I don't know."

"Go on. Decide."

"I don't know," said Minnie again. She looked as if she were going to cry. She never liked to have to make up her mind by herself. "You choose for me, Hetty."

Suddenly Hetty turned around to Aunt Molly, who was watching them from the parlor doorway.

"Aunt Molly—" she said.

"Take your time," said Aunt Molly. 'It's Papa's cabinet. He said you could have anything."

"But I like it better here," blurted Hetty, not exactly understanding what she meant herself. "I don't want to take anything away. Oh, Aunt Molly, what I want is for Tom and Caddie and Clara and Warren to see it—just like it is."

"Why, that's easy," said Aunt Molly. "Bring them over tomorrow."

"Aunt Molly, they're outside now. If they were very quiet—"

"Dear me!" said Aunt Molly. "They're outside? Of course they may come in."

Little Minnie was smiling now, too.

"And they never saw Adelaide, either, did they, Hetty?"

"No," said Hetty.

"Well, Henrietta, go and call them in, child."

"*Henrietta!*" thought Hetty.

Once the others were all in the house, grown-up Henrietta Woodlawn would be gone again and only Hetty would be left. And yet tonight, on Christmas eve, it was worth losing that other self to see the older brothers and sisters drinking in the wonders of the cabinet.

Hetty ran to the kitchen door to call them, and her heart was thumping hard with happiness.

This exerpt is from Magical Melons, *one of the Caddie Woodlawn books. This series was based on the stories told to the author by her grandmother, Caddie Woodhouse, whose family came from Boston in the 1850's. Their farm was 12 miles south of Menomonie. Carol Brink wrote numerous other children's stories as well.*

My First Christmas Tree

by Hamlin Garland

I will begin by saying that we never had a Christmas tree in our house in the Wisconsin coulee; indeed, my father never saw one in a family circle till he saw that which I set up for my own children last year. But we celebrated Christmas in those days, always, and I cannot remember a time when we did not all hang up our stockings for "Sandy Claws" to fill. As I look back upon those days it seems as if the snows were always deep, the night skies crystal clear, and the stars especially lustrous with frosty sparkles of blue and yellow fire—and probably this was so, for we lived in a northern land where winter was usually stern and always long.

I recall one Christmas when "Sandy" brought me a sled, and a horse that stood on rollers—a wonderful tin horse which I very shortly split in two in order to see what his insides were. Father traded a cord of wood for the sled and the horse cost twenty cents—but they made the day wonderful.

Another notable Christmas Day, as I stood in our front yard, midleg-deep in snow, a neighbor drove by closely muffled in furs, while behind his seat his son, a lad of twelve or fifteen, stood beside a barrel of apples, and as he passed he hurled a glorious big red one at me. It missed me, but bored a deep, round hole in the soft snow. I thrill yet with the remembered joy of burrowing for that delicious bomb. Nothing will ever smell quite as good as that Winesap of Northern Spy or whatever it was. It was a wayward impulse on the part of the boy in the sleigh, but it warms my heart after more than forty years.

We had no chimney in our home, but the stocking-hanging was a ceremony nevertheless. My parents, and especially my mother, entered into it with the best of humor. They always put up their own stockings or permitted us to do it for them—and they always laughed next morning when they found potatoes or ears of corn in them. I can see now that my mother's laugh had a tear in it, for she loved pretty things and seldom got any during the years that we lived in the coulee.

When I was ten years old we moved and prospered in such ways that our stockings always held toys of some sort, and even my mother's stocking occasionally sagged with a simple piece of jewelry or a new comb or brush. But the thought of a family tree remained the luxury of millionaire city dwellers; indeed it was not till my fifteenth or sixteenth year that our Sunday school rose to the extravagance of a tree, and it is of this wondrous festival that I write.

The land about us was only partly cultivated at this time, and our district schoolhouse, a bare little box, was set bleakly on the prairie; but the Burr Oak schoolhouse was not only larger, but it stood beneath great oaks as well and possessed the charm of a forest background through which a stream ran silently. It was our chief social center. There of a Sunday a regular preacher held "Divine service" with Sunday school as a sequence. At night—usually on Friday nights—the young people met in "ly-ceums," as we called them, to debate great questions or to "speak pieces" and read essays; and here it was that I saw my first Christmas tree.

I walked to that tree across four miles of moonlit snow. Snow? No, it was a floor of diamonds, a magical world, so beautiful that my heart still aches with the wonder of it and with the regret that it has all gone—gone with the keen eyes and the bounding pulses of the boy.

Our home at this time was a small frame house on the prairie almost directly west of the Burr Oak grove, and as it was too cold to take the horses out my brother and I, with our tall boots, our visored caps, and our long woolen mufflers, started forth afoot defiant of the cold. We left the gate on the trot, bound for a sight of the glittering unknown. The snow was deep and we moved side by side in the grooves made by the hoofs of the horses, setting our feet in the shine left by the broad shoes of the wood sleighs whose going had smoothed the way for us. Our breaths rose like smoke in the still air. It must have been ten below zero, but that did not trouble us in those days, and at last we came in sight of the lights, in sound of the singing, the laughter, the bells of the feast.

It was a poor little building without tower or bell and its low walls had but three windows on a side, and yet it seemed very imposing to me that night as I crossed the threshold and faced the strange people who packed it to the door. I say "strange people," for though I had seen most of them many times they all seemed somehow alien to me that night. I was an irregular attendant at Sunday school and did not expect a present, therefore I stood against the wall and gazed with open-eyed marveling at the shinng pine which stood where the pulpit was wont to be. I was made to feel the more embarrassed by reason of the remark of a boy who accused me of having forgotten to comb my hair.

This was not true, but the cap I wore always matted my hair down over my brow, and then, when I lifted it off, invariably disarranged it completely. Nevertheless I felt guilty—and hot. I don't suppose my hair was artistically barbered that night—I rather guess Mother had used the shears—and I can believe that I looked the half-wild colt that I was; but there was no call for that youth to direct attention to my unavoidable shagginess.

I don't think the tree had many candles, and I don't remember that it glittered with golden apples. But it was loaded with presents, and the girls coming and going clothed in bright garments made me forget my own looks—I think they made me forget to remove my overcoat, which was a sodden thing of poor cut and worse quality. I think I must have stood agape for nearly two hours listening to the songs, noting every motion of Adoniram Burtch and Asa Walker as they directed the ceremonies and prepared the way for the great event—that is to say, for the coming of Santa Claus himself.

A furious jingling of bells, a loud voice outside, the lifting of a window, the nearer clash of bells, and the dear old saint appeared (in the person of Stephen Bartle) clothed in a red robe, a belt of sleigh bells, and a long white beard. The children cried out, "Oh!" The girls tittered and shrieked with excitement, and the boys laughed and clapped their hands. Then "Sandy" made a little speech about being glad to see us all, but as he had many other places to visit, and as there were a great many presents to distribute, he guessed he'd have to ask some of the many pretty girls to help him. So he called upon Betty Burtch and Hattie Knapp—and I for one admired his taste, for they were the most popular maids of the school.

They came up blushing, and a little bewildered by the blaze of publicity thus blown upon them. But their native dignity asserted itself, and the distribution of the presents began. I have a notion now that the fruit upon the tree was mostly bags of popcorn and "corny copias" of candy, but as my brother and I stood there that night and saw everybody, even the rowdiest boy, getting something we felt aggrieved and rebellious. We forgot that we had come from afar—we only knew that we were being left out.

But suddenly, in the midst of our gloom, my brother's name was called, and a lovely girl with a gentle smile handed him a bag of popcorn. My heart glowed with gratitude. Somebody had thought of us; and when she came to me, saying sweetly, "Here's something for you," I had not words to thank her. This happened nearly forty years ago, but her smile, her outstretched hand, her sympathetic eyes are vividly before me as I write. She was sorry for the shock-headed boy who stood against the wall, and her pity made the little box of candy a casket of pearls. The fact that I swallowed the jewels on the road home does not take from the reality of my adoration.

At last I had to take my final glimpse of that wondrous tree, and I well remember the walk home. My brother and I traveled in wordless companionship. The moon was sinking toward the west, and the snow crust gleamed with a million fairy lamps. The sentinel watchdogs barked from lonely farmhouses, and the wolves answered from the ridges. Now and then sleighs passed us with lovers sitting two and two, and the bells on their horses had the remote music of romance to us whose boots drummed like clogs of wood upon the icy road.

Our house was dark as we approached and entered it, but how deliciously warm it seemed after the pitiless wind! I confess we made straight for the cupboard for a mince pie, a doughnut and a bowl of milk!

As I write this there stands in my library a thick-branched, beautifully tapering fir tree covered with the gold and purple apples of Hesperides, together with crystal ice points, green and red and yellow candles, clusters of gilded grapes, wreaths of metallic frost, and glittering angels swinging in ecstasy; but I doubt if my children will ever know the keen pleasure (that is almost pain) which came to my brother and to me in those Christmas days when an orange was not a breakfast fruit, but a casket of incense and of spice, a message from the sunlands of the South.

That was our compensation—we brought to our Christmastime a keen appetite and empty hands. And the lesson of it all is, if we are seeking a lesson, that it is better to give to those who want than to those for whom "we ought to do something because they did something for us last year."

Successful author of short stories, novels, and plays at the turn of the century, Hamlin Garland was born in West Salem, Wisconsin. He spent his youth in a variety of midwestern settings, Wisconsin, Iowa, Illinois, and South Dakota, before moving East to find literary success chronicling the often bleak life of the western frontier following the Civil War.

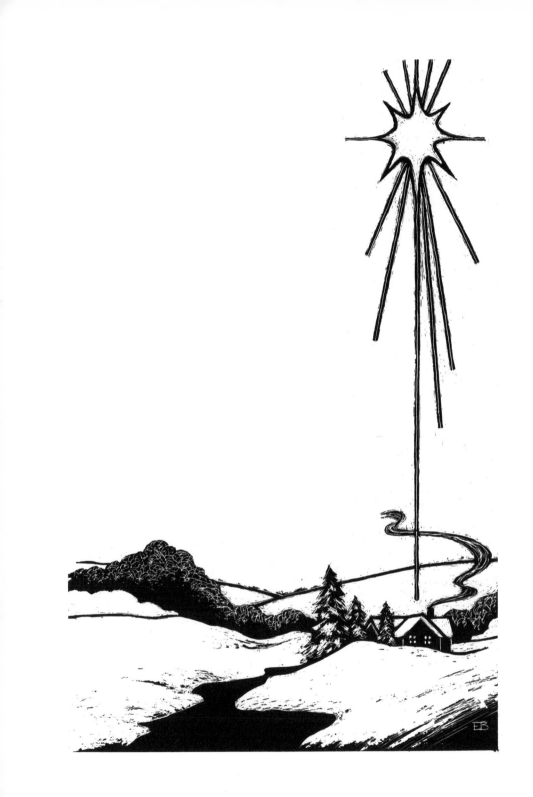

Keeping Christmas
Then and Now

Advice to Settlers

"Merry Christmas to You" is what we now hear from all as we plod by that milepost of time called "Christmas." We thank you sincerely, and would intrude a few thoughts that have arisen (from the Chair). Although Christmas is not the time at which you have been accustomed to receive advice, still, you may need a little just now.

Let not temporary discomfort cast a shadow over the time to be "merrie." These holidays will bring to our minds the ringing of bells, the still more pleasant chime of voices we love to hear, and the welcomes and wishes for future happiness that former days have seen; and we may well cherish these recollections. Yes, we may well cherish them; not to encourage homesickness and despondency but as a bright example for imitation, at the present.

Let us then wreath this season with the flowers we can gather from its predecessors, and cheer the Old Year with the smiles and respect due to his age.

On behalf of our friends here, and ourselves we send to those friends absent and abroad the kindly wishes that will doubtless more particularily expressed in their own words. And we hope to receive from the same, consideration to the memory of the "pioneers." As you gather round the Christmas tree think of us kindly; and we will do the same. And may there ever be a Christmas tree in our hearts, green and flourishing, from the ground of a generous soul, and its fruit of joy, thanksgiving, and love shall renew ourselves and those around us.

Eau Claire *Times*, December 19, 1851

77

More than 70 years after the fact Judge Elisha W. Keyes, Republican party leader, recalled his first Christmas after moving to Wisconsin territory from Vermont in September, 1837.

Frontier Christmas, 1837
by Judge E. W. Keyes

We had made our landing and transfer from the shanty to the new log house about the first week in December. It was certain now that the cheer of Christmas was to be vouchsafed to us. . . .

On that day all unnecessary work was suspended. In the evening a Methodist circuit rider dropped in upon us and gave us a word of hope and cheer. In that early day every loghouse occupied by a family was visited by one of these untiring men bent on the mission of carrying the gospel into the wilderness.

Now a great question confronted us! Out of what material was the Christmas feast to be prepared. The country was full of game, almost every species, but our hunters were not skilled. The deer fled and the prairie chickens were distant and not inclined to close companionship; the ducks and wild geese had gone southward; wild turkeys were rare, although a few were domiciled in this section. Our larder was lean and almost desolate. There was pork in one barrel, a little flour in another, and a small bag of Indian (corn) meal. So the pork and flour fulfilled the purposes and my mother having smuggled a few dried apples in the removal, an apple pie was the consequence, and O, how good it was! No stockings hung by the fireplace, no presents were given and none expected. The gifts that passed were those from heart to heart, and uppermost in the thoughts of all was the wish that there would dawn upon us a day of great splendor, when the territory as a state would be filled with teeming millions of people of the highest civilization. . . .

Lake Mills Leader, 1909

Kenosha Christmas, 1859
by Mary Bradford

Christmas was observed, but not so elaborately as today. There was no fireplace in our little home such as were found in old ancestral homes in the East, and in some larger Western homes and in public places. The best we could do to accommodate Santa Claus was to hang our stocking on a line behind the kitchen stove. Early Christmas morning found us examining the contents. There was one package which we always found at the top, and we knew what was in it before it was opened—a Christmas Cooky! This special cooky was a regular part of the Christmas program. Those I remember were of generous size and thickness, and were always decorated in an interesting way. They were covered on top with frosting, in which were stuck small candies of different colors, some of which, I remember, contained caraway seeds. There was always a centerpiece on this cooky. Sometimes it was a pink or white candy heart, with a motto such as "I love you" or "My girl" printed on it; and sometimes a turtle was stuck fast in the sweet, hard icing—a turtle that had a big raisin for a body, with legs of cloves protruding from it, and with another one for a head. After this cooky came sticks of candy, and a red apple, not one of those from our own orchard, in barrels and boxes in our cellar, but of a different sort, probably brought from town. There were striped sticks of candy and sometimes an orange was found, also, this was being a rare treat. Down in the stocking foot, carefully wrapped up was another package, as regularly there as the cooky on top. This was a bunch of large raisins, pressed flat from packing, but still attached to the stems. Most of the stocking contents were, as you see, edible, but a pair of mittens might sometimes be found among them. When the stockings were not hung, we found a package by our bedsides when we awoke, or by our plates at the breakfast table.

I was three years old and my youngest sister a baby, when the family had the first Christmas tree. We owed that to Katie, a German girl, who was our "hired girl" that winter. Katie was the daughter of a newly-arrived family, well educated and of fine stock. My mother undertook to teach English to Katie, and Katie reciprocated by teaching German to my mother. She was good natured and full of fun, and the family enjoyed her very much. The desciption of the Christmas eve of 1859 was often repeated in the family circle, and thus became familiar to me. Mother and Katie were busy in the kitchen with preparations for the next day; two geese had been chosen from the barnyard flock to furnish the most important item of the dinner. Father was persuaded that he could help most by going into the living room and putting the babies to sleep. He heard laughter and joking going on in the kitchen, and decided to see what it was all about; so he peeked through a knot-hole in the door. He saw Katie take the heads of the geese, wrap each in paper, and thrust them into the toes of his tall boots that stood behind the kitchen stove. Then followed the yellow legs and feet of the geese, also carefully wrapped in paper; and twigs of wood of the size of sticks of candy. This was all done with much giggling on Katie's part, as she pictured the surprise of father, when he thrust his feet into his boots in the morning. Morning came. Katie was busy with getting breakfast, but keeping watch of father's action. Taking his boots, he first took out the sticks of candy and presented them to the astonished girl; then came the packages of legs, with, "There are the legs, Katie,"—and with increased astonishment, she finally got the heads! By that time Katie was sure that mother had spoiled her fun by telling father what to expect, and it was only when the knot-hole was pointed out that she understood how father was "wise to her plan."

The children had helped the day before Christmas to get the tree ready. Since our woods had no evergreen trees, the boys had had to go to a farmer living some distance away to procure one, and had brought it home in a sleigh. It was set up in the living room on a table, placed against the outer doorway. The children helped to string the popcorn, and mother with Katie's help, made cookies cut into animal shapes, and others like the now famous "Gingerbread Boy" of the story. These were hung on the tree with as bright apples as could be found; tallow candles cut into short lengths were carefully wired to the branches. There were no tinsel ornaments or bright baubles, or safe little electric bulbs such as we have now for Christmas trees, but when on Christmas eve father lit the candles, it was a beautiful sight. Before it was put away, all the children of the neighborhood had seen our wonderful tree, and as long as the jar of cookies lasted, shared with us that part of the celebration.

Letters to Home at Christmas
by Caja Munch

Caja Munch came to Wiota, Wisconsin from Norway with her husband, Johan Munch, who had been sent as a minister to the Lutheran congregation. These letters to her family were collected and saved in Norway. The Munches and their two daughters born in Wisconsin left the state in 1859 and returned to their homeland. Her Norwegian descendants translated and published these letters in a book, The Strange American Way.

The First Year, Christmas 1856

Beloved Parents!

The day, indeed, has drawn to a close, but such a strong longing came over me to talk to you although I am so far, far away from you;

It has been a strange Christmas for me. On Christmas Eve we all had rice porridge, roast beef, and Christmas cookies together with Even and a man and his wife and a little child, who are staying here in the house. Afterwards we said our prayers and a sang a hymn and thought of our dear ones at home, who already by that time were sound asleep. You will recall that you are six hours ahead of us in time, which is hard on us sometimes, especially on such holidays when I wish so much for our thoughts to meet, but then it has to be worked out by calculation. Oh, how often have I not taken the watch and figured out what you were doing during the joyful Christmas time.

On the First Day of Christmas, I was with my dear Munch. He gave a beautiful sermon in his main church, but it was so cold that both words and thoughts were almost frozen away, although we lit a fire in the stove in the church. On the way home I wanted to run to keep myself from freezing but tripped in my black silk dress and tore it, but not too much—uh! You will have to be informed about everything, dear Mother, good and bad.

On the Second Day of Christmas, he went early in the morning to *Jallerston* [Yellowstone] and did not return until the Third Day. On the Fourth Day of Christmas we had supper with our nearest neighbor, Hans Haug. And bright and early on the Fifth Day, my dear Munch went with our good friend Ole Monssen to Dodgeville, from where he will not return until tomorrow evening. I wanted to go with him, but the weather turned too bad and cold. At present the roads are good, and the weather has been nice the last two days. For the winter Munch has rented an old bearskin coat from a man here, and I put on him everything I possibly can, but it certainly takes a lot to protect yourself from the cold here. Only those who have traveled in these parts can have any idea about the cold wind that blows over the prairie.

The Second Year, Christmas 1857

Our Yuletide entertainments are soon recounted. They consisted of reading and hearing the Word of God, all possible peace and comfort at home, thinking of Norway and all our beloved friends there, besides singing Norwegian patriotic songs, our wedding song, and other snatches that we would think of.

Emil, unfortunately, did not come to us for Christmas, the roads were so bad, and the weather cold; Munch's horses had to go to Dodgeville, and to hire another team was much too expensive. Besides, we had a very nice letter from him a few days ago, telling us that he was so busy with two newspapers to be printed between Christmas and New Year that it was impossible for him to come, otherwise he would have walked, which I now in a long letter to him strictly advised against for another time.

The Holmens, who are living in the little town of Linden, and whom I think I have described to you before, had promised to come and see us during Christmas, but since Munch did not get up there because of a mishap with the sleigh, we were afraid they would not come; partly for this reason and partly to announce the next divine service for New Year's Day, we got two boys to drive up there with Munch's horses and a borrowed sleigh. They were to return the next day, the day before Christmas Eve, but they did not arrive. Christmas Eve went by, and still they did not come. By this time we were almost certain they had frozen to death on the prairies, and we had a very dismal Christmas Eve. Munch and all three of our servants went to church Christmas Day, I stayed at home alone with the baby. Munch was not very happy and could not at all get into the proper solemn mood because he was thinking of the boys; one of them was one of his confirmants and had twice before gone with him the same road. Their parents came here and were very downhearted. But just as I was sitting down, in came not only the boys but also Madam Holmen with her two children. Her husband was unable to come until a few days later as he could not leave the store, which was kept open both Christmas Day and Boxing Day; there you see how the Americans observe the great Christmas Holidays. They had had much trouble on the way and had to stay overnight because of impassable roads, but God be praised that they returned safely, and you can imagine here was joy.

Indeed, we have a hard winter again this year, a lot of snow, storms, and freezing weather, and under such conditions it is almost impossible to go anywhere. Boxing Day, as Munch was going to one of his annex parishes, his horses went off the road and waded in snow to their ears. Snowplows are unheard of in this country, and to get into a blizzard on the prairies is attended with danger of life. The roads are then drifted over so completely that there is no trace of them, and it may happen that one drives around a circle without knowing where he will arrive. It is not uncommon that people freeze to death in their sleigh, and the horses arrive in town with dead bodies sitting frozen stiff in the sleigh, holding the reins. Last year it happened that a carriage stopped outside an inn, where the horses regularly used to rest, but as nobody came inside, the innkeeper went out, and lo! there were five persons sitting inside the carriage, and the driver in his box holding the reins, completely frozen and dead. However, this is due to their own carelessness, and I don't feel nearly as sorry for them as for the poor cows, pigs, sheep, and other small animals; what these poor creatures suffer when the weather is that cold cannot be described, for they seldom have as much as a bush under which to seek shelter. Although we have a stable to put them in, they still suffer from cold because it is so open that the snow drifts right in at them. On the Sixth Day of Christmas, the Holmens left, and the following day Munch went away, so now I am alone with the baby.

The Third Year, Christmas 1858

I had a lot of butchering done for Christmas, which I enjoyed doing—I seemed to live over again the old days in my home. Everything turned out well. I made almost all the things you prepare, dear Mother, although I did make some kind of meat sausage which I marvel that we never thought of cooking at home. I had to make black pudding for Munch, he likes it so well, and I had the pleasure of treating my dear Emil and Munch to delicious things for a long time. My baking for Christmas consisted of wort-cake, Christmas bread, flead-cakes, hartshorn pastry, and apple pie. I finished everything early, and we had a quiet, peaceful, wonderful Christmas Eve and Holiday Season. During this time, Munch visited only the nearest parishes, from where he returned the same day. He married one of his best friends after Christmas, Emil and I went to the wedding. The next day, we had four or five families in for dinner.

I find that this letter has a strange, brief style, but for the moment I am not capable of doing any better. The reason for it may be that for so long now I have been staying within these four walls, without seeing or hearing another well-bred person. A couple of days ago, Munch and Emil drove down to Dietrichson's, but I could not come along as the roads were very bad.

We are having a strange winter this year, no snow, no frost— may God bring us a healthy summer!

Christmas in Long Coulee Valley
by Thomas Pederson

The early pioneers brought all the old country's (Norway's) customs with them. Two weeks before the day, they commenced making preparations to celebrate the great event. I am afraid it wasn't so much in honor of the Savior born to mankind, as it was the anticipation of a long holiday free from labor, full of gaiety, and with all they could eat and drink of the best that could be produced. For be it known, *Jul* consisted not of one day as it does with us, but of thirteen days, and some even added one more before the celebration finally ended. No labor of any kind, except feeding the stock, could be done until after New Year. The first three days of Christmas were considered too holy for any gaiety. If anyone could not get to church, a sermon must be read by the head of the family while all other members sat around listening. But when the three days were up, then the real *Yulefest* started with parties and dances. A deep rooted respect for the Christian holiday kept everybody within the bounds of decency. There were no wild parties, but all enjoyed themselves to the uttermost while it lasted. . . .

In my early days many customs connected with that *Jul* gaiety were still in vogue. Prominent among them was the custom of what was called "going *Julebukk*." This consisted in dressing up in the most grotesque and fantastic manner that we could invent, put a mask over our faces, and go around from house to house as long as any one was up. It was always done evenings, and nearly always by young people, the greater the number the better. We would sneak up to the house, rap at the door and when it was open, burst in, often filling the room. We would then parade around the room a few minutes, giving inmates a chance to identify us if they could, but never daring to talk lest they would recognize our voices. I never knew the origin or meaning of this custom, but I do know that we had lots of fun.

The parties and dances were mostly for the younger set, the older people using these two weeks mostly for visiting each other. Through any other part of the year the steady grind of making a living and opening up a farm did not give any time for visiting, so now through these holidays they made up for it. Those who in the old country had been near neighbors and close friends, but here lived miles apart, would now come in whole sleigh loads and visit for several days. Then likely as not when the visit was over, those who had been hosts would get into their sleighs and follow their friends home for a stay of several days. Invitations for these long visits had perhaps gone out and been accepted months before, so they were seldom surprise visits, otherwise it would often have been well-nigh impossible in those cramped quarters to receive so many guests at a time. The pure friendship and the hospitality of those early set-tlers are something rarely found today. "Peace on earth, good will toward men" reigned supreme through those well earned holidays.

A Yule Fest

by Thurine Oleson

During the Christmas holidays, my folks always had a real party. Then everyone would drink the malt beer and homemade wine that Mother had made, and eat of all the good food she had been preparing for weeks. Then they would talk about Norway, and after a while it would get pretty lively. The men would, at least. If the downstairs of our little house got too crowded, the men would take off to the upstairs where they could smoke and drink and play cards in peace. They played mostly euchre and pedro, I never heard that there was any gambling amongst our people.

Since nearly every family had from seven to twelve children, it was an unusual child who couldn't find a partner her own age. When Uncle Ole Boe and Aunt Aslaug came, I would take Anne, and my sister Sena would take Signe and Gurina. The boys would have John and Henry, and in their youth, Andres, who later died of smallpox. These friendships kept up all our lives, some for ninety-five years.

The malt beer that Mother served so freely was made of hops, malt, syrup of molasses, and water according to the other ingredi-ents. They made the malt themselves, out of barley. It was first wet, then laid in a dry warm place until it started to sprout. After the malt was made, it was boiled with other ingredients, then strained and yeast added to make the brew "work" for a few days. She then skimmed off the yeast and put the brew in kegs. This crude beer was just a mild drink. You could take any amount of it and never even get lightheaded.

Civil War Christmas, 1864

The young pines, growing among the larger ones, were just such little trees as were used at home for Christmas trees, and within an hour after getting the camp made, every man thought of Christmas at home.

The boys went off in the woods and got holly and mistletoe, and every pup tent in the whole regiment was decorated, and they hung nose bags, grain sacks, army socks and pants on the trees. Around the fires, stakes had been driven to hang clothes on to dry; and as night came and the pitch pine fires blazed up to the tops of the great pines, it actually looked like Christmas, though there was not a Christmas present anywhere.

After supper the Brigade band began to play patriotic airs, with occasionally an old fashioned tune, like 'Old Hundred,' and the woods rang with music from the boys who could sing, and everybody was as happy as I ever saw a crowd of people, and when it came time to retire the band played 'Home Sweet Home,' and three thousand rough soldiers went to bed with tears in their eyes, and every man dreamed of the dear ones at home, and many prayed that the home ones might be happy, and in the morning they all got up, stripped the empty stocking off the evergreen trees, put them on, and went on down the road."

G. W. Peck, *How George W. Peck Put Down The Rebellion*

Christmas in Camp

Our Christmas dinner consisted of a few Irish potatoes and a little fresh beef. After dinner we sat around a campfire which was in front of our tent and talked of old times, each one telling where he was and what he was doing in years gone by on this day. Midnight and all is quiet. Thus ends Christmas day in the army at Pascagoula, Mississippi.

from the diary of John Buckly Bacon of Columbus, Wisconsin
December 25, 1864

Another Perspective

Christmas is a day of feasting both with white and black people. Those slaves who are lucky enough to have a few shillings are sure to spend them for good eating; and many a turkey and pig is captured, without saying, "by your leave, sir." Those who cannot obtain these, cook a 'possum, or a racoon from which savory dishes can be made. My grandmother raised poultry and pigs for sale; and it was her established custom to have both a turkey and a pig roasted for Christmas dinner.

Harriet A. Jacobs, *Incidents in the Life of a Slave Girl, 1860*

Memories of Christmas at the Wade House

In 1844 Sylvanus and Betsy Wade journeyed from New England to the wilderness of western Sheboygan County. They constructed an inn and had a large family and watched their area be transformed into a village reminiscent of the New England they had left. In 1869 the family gathered for the holidays as recalled by the Wade's granddaughter in her memoirs.

The Christmas I was 8 years old Grandma's children planned a surprise party for her, and Mamma cautioned us not to act as tho' we were expecting anyone. Finally a bobsled, drawn by horses with sleigh bells ringing merrily, drove up to the front door. All the children and their families who lived in Fond du Lac came tumbling out of robes and blankets and unloaded everything for a complete

Christmas dinner. They brought among other goodies, a pineapple for Grandma; the first such fruit I had ever seen. And Aunt Emma and Aunt Allie made ice cream in the old type freezer, giving me my first taste of ice cream. That eve they danced in the ballroom to the music of violins played by Grandpa and Uncle Hollis.

Jennie Hamilton Root

The Wade House has been restored by the State Historical Society and annually recreates a Yankee-style Christmas at Greenbush for the public.

Lumberjack's Christmas

by Otis W. Terpening

For two weeks before the great day, things took on a brighter hue, at least they seemed to. The lads were better natured than usual. And why shouldn't they be. Some had left their families and kiddies early in the fall, with the understanding that at Christmas they would all be united again, while others thought of the sweetheart back in the settlement. Then we had a kind with us that I can't describe in this up to date language. But us Jacks called them lushers: a class that was shunned by the better class of lumberjacks. For the only thing they seemly thought of getting out of life was a big drunk and a feed of ham and eggs. As there was no drinking allowed in camp, it was real hard on them.

And they all seemed to hail Christmas as a time of getting out of their bondage. As the day drew near the real Christmas Spirit seemed to prevail. And in the snatches of song that we would hear in the woodland during the day there was a real ring of joy in them. And in the voice of the Jacks on Christmas morning as they wished one another Merry Christmas. And to hear one Jack say, 'Thanks, Pal, I hope you live forever and I live to see you die.' We seldom ever worked on Christmas, but the day was spent in visiting, darning our socks and mittens. While some spent their time in playing cards and listening for the cheerie sound of the dinner horn, saying come and eat, eat. The cook would always have something extra, and plenty of it.

There was roast beef, brown gravy, good home-made bread, potatoes, shiny tins heaped with golden rings called fried cakes, and close to them a pumpkin pie baked in a ten-inch tin, about one-and-a-half-inch deep, and cut in four pieces. Any other day to a Jack it was one piece, but today it was Christmas. It only came once a year and help yourself, if you wanted a whole pie you was welcome. And rice pudding black with raisins, dried prunes, or the old-fashioned dried apples for sauce. Black coffee sweetened with brown sugar. And tins full of sweet cookies. They were white and had a raisin in the center of them. Did we eat, I will say we did! I have eaten many a Christmas dinner in camp. And some here on the farm, but the best was in camp. Just one more with a jolly crew, and I would be willing to say, 'Life is now complete.'

After Christmas dinner—which was served at noon—the loggers relaxed until it was time for supper, which was almost a repeat of the main repast. Some would get out the old greasy deck of cards and climb into some pal's top bunk for a quiet game of poker, while others took to the old-time square dances. The 'ladies' had a grain sack tied around their waist so we could tell them from the gents. And woe to the one that stepped on a lady's toe, and did not apologize. And do it quick. Or it would be one quick blow and a Jack would measure his length on the floor. Then it was the first two gents cross over and by the lady stand. The second two cross and all join hands. And we had to have a jig every set.

Applejack Cider

In a large pot combine:

> 1 gallon apple cider
> 1/3 cup brown sugar
> 1 six-ounce can frozen orange juice
> 1/4 cup lemon juice
> 6 Constant Comment tea bags

Bring to a slow boil. Pour into hearty-sized mugs then add as much applejack brandy as your tastes and spirit desire.

American Cub, Kohler

Christmas Tree

by Robert Peters

Wednesday morning, December 20th. Shimmering trees were loaded with ice. My sister and I were dressed for the outdoors. "Get one with a good shape," my mother said. "And be careful with that axe."

We rushed on skis over the packed trail, crossing fields, the south pasture, and on through birch and tamarack to the lake. Fresh rabbit tracks had broken the ice crust. I carried the axe. We whirred along for half an hour and then we halted before a superb view of frozen Minnow Lake.

I shook a tree, a flaring spruce, freeing it of snow. It chopped easily. I tied a rope around it and secured the rope to my waist. "OK," I said. "You lead, Margie." The tree slid easily over the ski trail. We are exhilarated—cutting the tree was the first event of Christmas.

I built a clumsy stand in the living room, away from the heater. The odor of crushed needles, saps, and resins was magnificent.

We had few ornaments: Of a dozen glass pieces, my favorites were a pair of multicolored, miniature bass viols, and a small glass deer, missing its antlers. We made chains from the colored pages of old magazines glued with paste made of flour, water, and salt. I enjoyed fitting the pink and red twisted wax candles in their metal holders to the branches. We lighted the candles.

We drew pictures for one another, to keep secret until Christmas morning. We had made presents for our mother: I decorated a box of safety matches with fancy paper taken from envelopes supplied by our teacher, and I carved a bar of Ivory soap into a squirrel. Miss Crocker sketched the animal, and I was near tears before I managed to whittle the creature free of the soap. Around it's neck I tied a small bit of green ribbon and a medallion saying "Squirrel." I hoped my mother would like it.

Robert Peters, a professor on the faculty of the University of California, has published more than twenty volumes of poetry as well as essays and literary criticism. This selection quoted is from Crunching Gravel, *a book relating his Wisconsin boyhood on a farm in Eagle River during the Depression.*

Season Within A Season

by Ben Logan

Even when I was very young, Christmas was a time of memory. It stretched back across the years, filled with all the kaleidoscopic rememberings of other Christmases, always moving us close together in a special time of loving and being loved. It reached back even beyond my own birth. I could see earlier Christmases in the way Mother hung a favorite, faded ornament on the tree, in the way Father's face softened when he began to sing a Christmas carol in Norwegian. Always one of my brothers would say, "Remember the time the dog knocked the tree down?" I couldn't remember, but I could see it. It became so much a part of Christmas that one year I beat everyone else and said it myself. No one realized that I only remembered through their remembering.

There was a tinseled star at the top of the tree, always speaking of ancient times and three wise men, reminding me of Father traveling across the wide sea, guided home by stars, lighthouses, and, now, by Mother's lamp burning in the kitchen window.

Christmas was, and is, lights and colors, warmth and laughter, remembered voices and all the sad and happy sounds of childhood. It is the feel of heavy brown wrapping paper, the tune of a music box with a bright yellow knob, the smell of pine pitch and of an orange being peeled. It is the first flash of the incredibly red dump truck I got when I was seven years old, the buttery smell of sugar cookies, the feel of the finely worked wool of a new turtle-neck sweater that no older brother had ever worn. It is the silvery tinkling sound of a candy wrapper as I unveiled a mysterious chocolate, then put the smoothed-out foil into an encyclopedia along with the faded flowers and bright candy wrappers from other years.

Christmas was a season within a season, filled with mystery and wonder. How could it be such a part of us, yet still seem to come from outside ourselves? How could it be new each year, yet always be the same Christmas, the way it is with an old and familiar tree that is always there, yet always has new growth?

I don't know the answers. I only know that each year we reached out to find Christmas and make it happen, and each year Christmas reached out and found us instead. It found us even in that strange winter we always spoke of as "the time we didn't have a Christmas tree."

The season began as usual. The last day of school came, and that was the first day of Christmas for us. Teacher, as always on that day, had a frantic look. We could not stay in our seats or keep from whispering.

Junior wasn't there, he was at home with a cough. When we came crashing into the kitchen, Father and Mother were talking about whether or not Junior should go to the school program that night. Junior was looking from one to the other as they talked, his face pale, eyes very big. He smiled when they decided it would be all right.

We did the chores before supper. Lyle finished the last half of his hot coffee in one noisy gulp and hurried out to get the horses and the big bobsled ready. With the yellow light of a lantern to show us the way, we went out to the sled. Lyle had filled the two-foot-high sled box with straw and put all our old blankets on top. Mother had heated several of her irons on top of the kitchen stove and brought them along, wrapped in old towels, in case anyone's feet got cold.

We blew out the lantern and climbed in, pulling blankets around us. Lyle was up front. He flipped the lines, said, "Gid-y-ep," and we glided out along the ridge to the west, the wind reaching for us, the tug chains ringing like bells behind the trotting horses.

Our eyes adjusted to the darkness. A faint blue light seemed to hang just over the surface of the snow. We could see the graceful roll of the drifts along the road, the smooth outline of snow-covered fields, the faint shadow of the next ridge to the north and beyond that the lights of Mount Sterling.

Father was wearing his old horsehair coat and had promised Mother he would leave it in the sled. Mother's hands were tucked deep into her big fur muff, holding it up to protect her face from the wind. Junior was huddled almost out of sight in Father's big sheepskin coat. The sled runners rattled sometimes when we hit crusted snow.

"Look!" Mother said, pointing.

There were glittering little pinpoints of light shining in a field where the wind had swept away the snow and uncovered patches of smooth ice.

"What are they?"

"The reflection of the stars," said Father.

We lay down on our backs, protected from the wind, sinking deep into the straw with its smell of summer, and we looked up at the distant stars.

"How many do you think there are?"

"A billion, I bet."

"A trillion."

"Eighty-nine thousand quadrillion."

"So many you could spend the rest of your life counting them and still not count them all."

"Is it always the same stars?"

"Of course it is."

"I mean if you tried to count them, would they all just stay there and be the same ones?"

"Hey, maybe there's stars that just visit us, maybe once every thousand years."

"Comets do that, not stars."

"Well, why shouldn't a star be able to do that if a comet can?"

"Shush," said Mother. "Just enjoy them."

We went on into the shelter of the woods. The wind was almost gone, the breath of the horses quick and white as they walked up the steep hill beyond the deep ravine. We topped the hill and turned down into the narrow school road, sled runners gliding silently through the undisturbed snow, bare limbs of trees so thick above us they almost shut out the stars. An owl hooted. Something quick and small, a rabbit maybe, scurried away from the road and vanished in the woods.

"There's the light," Lyle said as we came down into the little hollow that led to the schoolhouse. The runners of other sleds were rattling on the icy road beyond the creek. Horses were whinnying. Yellow lights bobbed up and down in the meadow east of the schoolhouse where people were coming on foot, carrying kerosene lanterns. We found a place between two other teams, tied up to the top rail of the fence, and Father and Lyle covered the horses with blankets.

The schoolhouse was warm, filled with the light and smell of a half dozen kerosene lamps. One was flickering. Mother smiled at me. "It needs you to trim the wick."

The big wreath we had made from pine limbs and bittersweet berries was hanging under the clock. The blackboard had hundreds of little dabs of chalk on it.

"I told you it wouldn't look like snow," Junior said when he saw the blackboard. His voice was a hoarse whisper. He stayed with Mother in a front seat, his hands tucked inside her muff. Soon the room was crowded, some people dressed "in their best bib and tucker," as Mother would say, some in work clothes that carried a barn smell through the warm room. There was a burst of laughter when a long-legged man tried to squeeze into the desk he'd used when he was in the eighth grade.

"Look," he said, pointing at the desk top, "there's my initials."

Several high-school boys stood at the back of the room, whispering and laughing. A girl near them got up, marched to the front, and crowded into another seat, her face as red as the ribbon in her hair.

Teacher welcomed everyone. Mostly she talked about how hard we had worked. I think she was asking people not to laugh at our mistakes.

We all trooped out of the cloakroom for our first number, jostled into position, and sang "Jingle Bells," almost everyone remembering to say "Bells on bob-tailed Ned."

The next number was "Scenes from an Early Wisconsin Christmas." The piano began. An Indian crept out, an arrow ready in his half-drawn bow. When his head feather slipped, he grabbed for it and the arrow went up in the air and came down on the piano keyboard, playing one sharp pinging note. The woman at the piano, I think her name was Elsie, slid over to the other end of the bench. It tipped and dumped her off. She reached up and went right on playing while she was getting up from the floor.

Tom Withers came in, crawling on all fours, playing a hungry bear. The Indian was supposed to shoot him, but he couldn't find his arrow. Tom ran in circles, one of them carrying him too close to the Christmas tree. His head went through a loop in a string of popcorn. Tom kept on going. The tree tipped and came down on top of him. He roared, as a bear or as himself we never knew, and galloped off with the string of popcorn following.

The audience did its best. People were able to control their laughter until a boy came out for the first lines of our scene.

"Christmas in early Wisconsin," he said, "was not an easy time."

"By God, you can say that again," boomed a voice from the back. "What with bears in the house and all."

The room filled with laughter. Men were pounding their legs and wiping tears out of their eyes. The women stopped first and began shushing everyone until it was quiet again.

A third-grader marched out to do her piece about Christmas fairies. After four sentences or so, she forgot her lines and switched over and did "The Village Blacksmith" instead. The audience applauded anyway and she walked off, head high, looking very pleased.

A boy did part of "Snowbound." I don't think he understood the opening lines because he always put a question mark after them. "The sun that cold December day, it sank from sight before it set?"

A girl began reciting "The First Snowfall." Halfway through, her little brother wandered up front and stood looking up at her. She went on speaking, shooing him away with her hands, but he stayed right beside her. She stopped for a minute, sighed, then took his hand and went on with the poem, the little boy beaming at her.

The girl took the little boy back to his seat and walked to the cloakroom. The audience was very quiet. Then the applause came, longer for that girl than for any other part of the program.

We all lined up and started singing "Joy to the World," but were interrupted by the sound of horses fighting. Half the men ran outside, and we waited, frozen in the middle of a line, until everyone came back. The piano started again at the beginning. We went on from where we were. At the end, an angel was supposed to walk across in front of us. One of her wings fell off. She tripped on it and said, in a clear whisper, "Darn! I told her it wouldn't stay on."

Everything else went all right unless you counted a key sticking on the piano and a man prying it up with his jackknife.

Warm, and so full of cocoa we could hear it sloshing when we wiggled our stomachs, we started home. Lanterns were going in all directions, the night filled with young and old voices.

"Merry Christmas!"

"Goodnight. Merry Christmas."

"See you in two weeks."

"Don't forget we're going to roll a big snowball."

We went up the road, Denny Meagher and his sister, Margaret, close behind us in their sled. We said "goodnight" and "Merry Christmas" to them, then turned out along Seldom Seen ridge by ourselves. The moon had come up. The trees made sharp black shadows on the snow. Mother began singing "Oh, Little Town of Bethlehem," her voice high and clear, getting lost out against the bright stars. Father's deep voice joined her, his Norwegian accent more noticeable when he was singing. We all sang, except Junior, as the horses trotted toward home.

We got out in front of the house and Lyle took the horses on to the barn. Junior was coughing, looking very white when Father carried him inside.

"Open the davenport," Mother said to Lee and me.

The davenport was in the living room. We opened it and Father put Junior down, then carried coals from the dining-room stove for a fire. Sticky from the popcorn balls and still working on the hard candy and peanuts, we went off to bed with two weeks of vacation ahead and plans enough to fill a year.

Junior was still sick next day and the day after that. The door to the living room stayed closed except when we tiptoed in to put more wood in the stove.

Dr. Farrell came from Seneca, bundled up in a big coat and a fur cap, riding in a little sleigh that we called a cutter. We ran out to take his horse.

"I'll give her some water and oats," Lyle said.

"You will, will you?" Dr. Farrell roared. He had a voice, Lyle liked to say, that was like a cream can full of walnuts rolling down a steep hill. The doctor headed for the house with his bag, then yelled over his shoulder, "By God, it's a help all right, having the horse taken care of."

We watched from the dining-room doorway while he warmed his stethoscope over the stove and listened to Junior's throat and chest. He left the thermometer in for a long time "'Cause it's cold as a damned icicle to start with!" When he read the thermometer, he came out into the dining room, closing the door behind him. Father and Mother were waiting.

"Scarlet fever," Dr. Farrell said.

"What does that mean?"

"Means he's going to be a mighty sick boy. Keep the other children out of that room. Be better if only one of you goes in there." He went on talking to Mother while we got his horse and hitched it to the cutter.

Junior kept getting worse, his fever so high we could hear him mumbling and talking in his sleep even with the door closed. Once he said in a loud, angry voice, "I said I wanted skis!"

It was a strange Christmas season. We didn't do any of the things we'd planned. Mother hardly had time to talk to us, except to tell us what needed to be done. Dr. Farrell came every day. Then, maybe four or five days before Christmas, Mother told us there wouldn't be a Christmas tree.

"We'll do something about it later, maybe. There just isn't enough time now. Anyway, the doctor says we have to keep the house quiet." She was almost crying when she went into the other room and closed the door.

"You help her all you can," Father said. "Don't wait to be asked."

"Is Junior going to get well?"

He looked at us for a long time. I used to wonder when he did that if he was thinking in Norwegian and had to change it back to English.

"We don't know," he said.

I don't remember how Laurance felt about what was happening, but Lee and I began to feel cheated. In the safe isolation of the big dark closet at the head of the stairs, we dared to come right out and tell each other there wasn't any Santa Claus. I'm sure we already knew it wasn't Santa who brought our presents, but he had gone on being a part of Christmas for a long time and we still believed in Christmas, all right. But what kind of a Santa Claus, even if he was just a "spirit," would let Junior get this sick at Christmastime?

We still ran to meet the mailman every day, hoping for packages, especially packages with revealing rattles or holes in them. One day George Holliday handed us one that didn't need a hole. He winked and laughed. "Here you are. What comes in a package four inches wide, five feet long, and curves up at one end?"

"Junior's new skis," we said.

"How is he?"

"Still sick."

"Well, when he gets his skis, he'll be better."

"He won't be getting them. We don't even have a Christmas tree."

"Well hell's bells," George said. "No wonder he's sick."

We took the skis to the house and gave them to Mother. She put them away. "He might not even know if I gave them to him."

Lee and I spent more and more time in the dark closet, trying to get Christmas to happen. All our other Christmases began to form in our minds as we talked. We always cut two or three branches from the white pine in the yard and tied them together to make a nice full tree. We hung all the ornaments, some of the tin ones old and dented. We put up the star and threaded popcorn and cranberries onto strings and draped them around the tree. There was a little package that unfolded and magically became a big red paper bell to hang over the dining-room table, so low we had to be careful not to put the lamp under it. On Christmas Eve we always turned the lamp down low and lighted the candles on the tree, Father watching from the kitchen door with a bucket of water in his hand. We would look at the burning candles and eat the little round candies with pictures in the center that were a promise of what was to come in the morning.

Christmas Day always began with the presents, but there was much more. Father would put out his sheaf of grain for the birds. There were navel oranges and bright red apples that made our own seem pale and small, and always a letter from Norway with a strange stamp, the envelope lined in brightly colored tissue paper. We'd all sit down and Father would tell us what the letter said, giving us a once-a-year glimpse of a grandmother and aunts and uncles who were only pictures in the old leather suitcase.

Soon, the smells of Christmas dinner would spread through the house, so strong and good we forgot our presents and gathered, starving, in the kitchen to hurry Mother along. Father said a blessing in Norwegian and we ate until we couldn't hold another bite, then ran around the table four times and ate some more.

After dinner Mother would bring out the package of books. Each year, just before Christmas, she sent off a letter to the State Lending Library, asking them to send us about thirty books for three adults and four boys. She gave our ages and a few words about each of us. She'd never let us read what she said, though sometimes she'd include our suggested additions, things like "Please don't send *Black Beauty* again this year." Then someone in the library in far-off Madison would read the letter and would, we liked to think, sit down, close their eyes, see us, and decide what books to send.

Only then, with everyone gathered in the warm house, with presents, books to read, and all the good things to eat, would Christmas have really come.

Lee and I could go back over all that in the closet, but this time it didn't happen. We ran into the dining room on Christmas morning and it was just like any other day, except that Mother looked sad and hollow-eyed and Father was walking restlessly around the room. Dr. Farrell came right after breakfast. We heard him say something about "today being a critical day."

When the doctor left, Mother brought out a present for each of us. They weren't wrapped with the usual bows and ribbons. I guess Father must have done them. Lee and I got the double-barrelled popguns we'd been wanting. Wondering how we could have missed a package that slim and long, we tore them out of the boxes, cocked them, and started to pull the double triggers. Father grabbed us.

"Better go outdoors with those."

We went out and tried target practice for a while, using twigs, corks, and pieces of ice for bullets. It began to snow, big wet flakes. We rolled giant snowballs, leaving paths of bare brown lawn behind us, and made a snowman, then used our new popguns to shoot marbles into his front for buttons.

It didn't feel like Christmas, even with the snow falling. We sat down with our backs against the snowman and waited for something to happen.

What happened was that a man we'd never seen before came walking along the road from the west. He was wearing a stocking cap and had a stick over his shoulder with a little bundle on the end. Sometimes tramps came by with a bundle like that, heading for the railroad along the Kickapoo River. The man saw us sitting there against the snowman and waved to us.

"Merry Christmas!" he called in a big voice.

We waved back, and he went on walking down the road with the snow falling around him.

We started talking about Junior and Christmas again. The first thing we decided was that Junior should get his skis. But we had to do more than that.

"We could say Santa Claus came by with them."

That wasn't going to be good enough for skeptical Junior.

What if somebody did come by? And saw us sitting here?"

"Yeah, somebody like an old man with a stocking cap and a bundle on his back."

"What if he asked how come we weren't happy and playing?"

"Yeah, and we said because our brother's sick."

"And maybe he'd be like Mr. Holliday. He'd say, 'No wonder he's sick. What you need to do is take him his present.' "

"And tell him he's going to be all right."

"Do you think he'd believe that?"

"Maybe the old man better have a beard."

"Yes, a red beard."

Dr. Farrell stopped by again and we followed him into the house. He came back out of the other room and said, "He's no better."

"Can we see him?" Lee asked.

Mother shook her head.

"We want to give him his skis."

Mother looked at Dr. Farrell. He sighed. "Oh, it can't hurt anything. But don't go up close. Stay away from the bed."

Mother got the skis. We unwrapped them and took them in, closing the door behind us. Junior was lying on his back, two pillows under his head. His eyes were open but he didn't look at us. He was making a funny noise when he breathed, and his freckles stood out very plain. He didn't even seem like Junior.

We held up the skis so he could see them. We started telling him about the old man.

Pretty soon Junior looked at us. When he started shaking his head a little bit, it was Junior all right.

"Tramp," he whispered.

"No, it wasn't! He had a long beard."

"A red one!"

Junior stopped shaking his head and seemed to be thinking about that. We shoved the skis onto the bed and pushed them up beside him. He took a deep breath and closed his eyes.

We tiptoed out.

"Did you give him the skis?"

"Yes. And he went to sleep."

Mother started for the other room. Dr. Farrell stopped her. He went in and closed the door. When he came out he looked surprised. "That's right. He is asleep. I think he's breathing better."

Mother hugged us. For the first time it seemed like Christmas.

Four or five days later, when Dr. Farrell came by, he said Junior could get up the next day. Mother smiled and said she thought maybe she'd go to bed when he got up. She looked at us. "I'm sorry about the tree."

"Hummp!" said Dr. Farrell. "Seems to me Christmas came anyway!"

Ben Logan, born in 1920 on a southwestern Wisconsin farm, attended the University of Wisconsin and Eastern schools. He lives in New York where he works in writing and production of film, radio, and television. He returns to his boyhood in two books, The Land Remembers *and* The Empty Meadow *which recount farm life along the Mississippi in Crawford County.*

Home Church Christmas
by Dave Engel

When I think of a church at Christmas, it often is of an old wooden church in a smaller town than this—the fundamentalist Evangelical United Brethren home church of my father and mother.

My impression of the building itself is of a simple, steepled structure.

I remember stained-glass windows donated "in loving memory of" and hard wooden pews in which the same people sat the same place every time I saw them, which was every time I went. Missing church on Sunday was unthinkable if not actually sinful.

It was not as clear to me then as it now is that the speech and demeanor of the parishioners is determined by their being German.

The white foreheads and rough hands tell me clearly, though, that they are farmers who work almost all the time, who abide close to earth and animals. The men and boys often smell of manure and silage, having been to the barn Sunday morning, as every morning, for chores. They wear the same simple, gray suits they always have worn.

A few are strangers to me. Many belong to my own family of uncles and aunts, cousins and grandparents. Others are elderly men and women I often meet at the church, whose relationship to me is obscure. They seem to be from another time. Some are children I don't really know.

Many of the Brethren are as strict as my own relatives. There is to be no drinking, no smoking and no card-playing. Social life seems to be a matter of restrained if good-humored sobriety. It's early to bed, early to rise.

Normally, we visit the old church by day but, at Christmas, we go at night.

On the snowy drive in from the farm, Mom leads carols, such as "Silent Night" and "Oh Holy Night." Alighting from Grandpa's Hudson at the church, Mom and Dad happily greet friends and family from way back when they too, lived here.

Young and old show genuine enthusiasm. For the children, there are treats to come. For the parents, the burden of husbandry has lifted. A more peaceful occupation shows in their faces.

The sanctuary has changed, too. With other lights dimmed, modest Christmas ornamentation and a tree have appeared. Figures on the windows reflect red and green light from within. An organist plays soft Christmas melodies rather than the more strident hymns of Sunday.

From somewhere on the left, I watch as darkness comes over the room and angels appear, their wings of gift cardboard and their coat-hanger halos just as amazing as feathers or fins.

Other children of farmers have changed into bathrobes. They carry staffs and wands, and have adopted a new tongue, speaking in terms like "behold" and "glad tidings" and "a king is born."

In the old church, among people who normally don't encourage a lot of fooling around, these children have got up to put on a show. To the little boy in the dark, it is more than prestidigitation.

Township Christmas

by Justin Isherwood

Christmas is the farmers' holiday. The reason is one of logistics. Memorial Day, Independence Day, and Labor Day all come at a time when farmers cannot take liberties with their vocation. That the rest of the nation celebrates makes little difference. Christmas, on the other hand, comes at a time when the fields lie frozen and resting from the marathon event of summer. Work has cooled its fevered pace; the mows, granaries, and warehouses attest to the green season's end.

Christmas is a time when, for a moment, we are all believers in magic. The selfish find themselves generous; the quiet find themselves singing. It is a time when people become a little crazy and take to hiding things in secret places. A time when country boys sneak to the barn on Christmas Eve and sit in the dark, waiting to hear cows speak in human tongues. A time when the weed pullers of summer walk their fields spreading thistle, sunflower, and rye seeds, hoping for a blessing flight of birds over their land in the belief that feathered prayers are best. A time when children leave a plate of cookies for the storied red-suited gentleman, an act uncharacteristic of sweet-toothed youngsters.

Remembered are all the knitted socks, caps, and mittens that mothers forced habitually on their children, despite the children's best efforts to lose, mutilate, or outgrow them. Remembered, too, are the flannel pajamas and the quilts stuffed with raw wool or old wedding suits. They were warm comfort in wood-heated, sawdust-insulated houses. As surely as people made these gifts, these gifts made the people.

Indeed, there were store-bought BB guns, toy trains that puffed flour smoke, Raggedy Ann dolls, and bicycles. There were baseball bats, Flexible Flyers, and ice skates. But beyond the store-bought were other contraptions, inventions of glue and jack plane, of countersunk screw and dovetail mortise. In the lingering warmth of the loving hands that made them, these were gifts that conveyed affection.

There were dollhouses with tiny doors and itsy-bitsy cupboards, even two-holers out back. Bookshelves and basswood mixing spoons, breadboards and spice racks. A coffee table with a purple blemish, testifying to the fence staple some great-grandfather had driven into the tree from which the table came. A child's wagon, its white-ash wheels turned on a basement lathe; a cradle with birch headboard; a dulcimer of prized black walnut. And a rocking chair, made from pine, pegged and glued. In it were lulled to sleep three generations of babies; in it were rocked away the anxious days of two world wars and one jungle fight.

There were even simpler gifts. A pancake breakfast shared with neighbors; the sudden appearance of two cords of oak firewood; snow tires mysteriously installed. Notes in the bottom of stockings promised two Sunday mornings of skipping church or three choreless Saturday mornings to go romp in the woods. Some notes promised simply to reveal a favorite fishing hole or a tree where flickers nested.

There was a gift, too, in all the cookies cut and made in the shape of angels and stars and reindeer. To children, it was a gift of powerful pride that they might decorate stars from their humble perch behind the steamed-up windows of a country kitchen.

A township Christmas was homegrown popcorn, spotted kernels of red and purple and bright yellow, shelled on the living-room floor, cobs tossed to the fire. It was hazelnuts to crack—by kids sitting cross-legged near the stove. It was ice-skating on the irrigation pit, with popple-branch hockey sticks and stone pucks. It was hot cider, suet pudding, black fudge, cranberry bread, and oyster stew.

And it was the tree brought home from the woodlot in the emptied honey wagon. That great green tree swelled the whole house with its vapors, its fragrance and good cheer, leaving few lives untouched by a simple act.

Christmas in the township still takes its cue from that generous bounty first given by the land. It was in just such a country place that angels were heard to sing of a child laid in a feedbox. It was, as all farmers know, a good place to be born.

Born in 1946 Justin Isherwood lives on the same family farm in Plove Township, south of Stevens Point, where he was raised. He is a frequent contributor to Wisconsin magazines; these essays have been collected in a volume entitled The Farm West of Mars.

Country Holidays
by Edward Harris Heth

The rewards are great for the country dweller when the winter holidays come. Holidays mean remembrance, of course, and the turkeys, stuffings, relishes and pies of one's own childhood are always better than any other. Out here there is the added pleasure of discussions with neighbors for weeks beforehand—which farmer will supply the best bird? There is the constant scanning of morning and evening skies as the special time approaches: snow would be perfect, but not too much to make driving hazardous for weekend guests coming to visit.

In the country, too, are the weeds, slim dark stalks of mullein and tawny milkweed pods, bright berries of bittersweet and garlands of ground pine to gather to decorate the house. There is the gusty wind at night, while you polish silver in the warm kitchen. Nuts from the woods are heaped in a chopping bowl, as they always were at my grandmother's house. Groceries are stacked everywhere; half the enjoyment of them is the trip to shop for them at the village store. Jellies and chutneys wait on the cupboard shelf. It is all prodigality and memory and custom. The stuffing and plate-sized slabs of white meat, the gravy, the preserves and dessert will taste exactly as they did years ago in my mother's house.

Then comes Christmas.

From Mrs. Brubaker wintering out in Arizona, there has already arrived the hoped-for gift of six precious jars of Eugene's stuffed, rum-soaked prunes, of which he brags all summer long, and well he might. A few relatives and friends arrive to spend the holidays and to help decorate the tree, not inside the house but out on the front terrace, hung with yards of tinsel and glittering ornaments, gold and silver, cut from tin cans saved all year. Seen through the living room windows at night, lit with green and amber light, it is stately and silent, the meadow black beyond it. It seems part of earth, not manmade.

The Stollen from Aunt Elsa is late in arriving—worrisomely, for homemade nut- and cherry-strewn Stollen for breakfast on Christmas morning has long been a tradition in my family. But one day the package is waiting in the post office in the village, along with a gift from the postmistress—a box of her homemade sugar plums (which I had thought were only the fantasy of some ancient storyteller's imagination, until I tasted one; hers is an old New England recipe). The Stollen, sugar plums, stuffed prunes are true Christmas presents, as is that of Father Quintana. After midnight Mass he ploughs through the snow in his station wagon like a speed-happy Magus, arriving with a generous gift of his own spicy, heady chutney. There is a late buffet waiting for him. Ham baked in a rye crust—baked for no special meal, but only to have on hand for guests at any time of night or day through the holidays; it is served sliced cold in thin curls on a big platter, drenched with a pome-granate sauce kept ready all Christmas week in the icebox. Beside it, since he likes sweets even at three o'clock in the morning after a good number of highballs (as do some of the less bibulous ladies) waits a punch bowl filled with a light and lovely old-fashioned dessert: blobs of merngue drifting on a lake of custard and called, as long as I can remember, Floating Island.

On Christmas morning the buttered Stollen is eaten while dozens of cups of coffee are consumed. The meadow is white and vast; the hills white and rolling. The Christmas dinner (turkey again) is in the oven. Some house guests are skiing; others, though thinking themselves less venturesome, are making far more perilous descents down the rocky hills in a coasting pan. But before dinner I pay calls on neighbors if I can sneak out between other neighbors paying calls on me. At the Barkers' I am handed a plate of almond-and-wine cakes, which Rosalie passes around accompanied by a chaste, gentle glass of her homemade dandelion wine (which has also gone into the cookies). Matt turns his drink down and glumly announces that they were just planning to call on me—at my house he gets Martinis.

At Ruth Hummock's across the road, I find a loud, cheerful, women's house because all her men, from the fourteen-year-old on up, have been down at the corner tavern since noon dinner. And here I collect more bounty—a half-gallon jar of homemade sauer-kraut and a dressed, frozen rooster which, she says with a husky but modest chuckle, she "had made into a capon especially." And still another gift: a friend of Ruth's, prosperous enough to winter in Florida, has sent them a crate of succulent, tree-ripened oranges. But Ruth's canned-juice-bred children won't eat them, saying they taste funny. And so, the case of marvelous and rare, really ripe and undyed fruit is loaded into my car. Ruth is relieved to have the odd things out of her kitchen shed.

Back home, some of my ex-city neighbors have dropped in. They look ruddy and bright. Helen has bought her husband, Mac, a new oil burner for Christmas for the old farmhouse they're remodeling. Mac, turned week-end painter since leaving town, has given Helen a gouache self-portrait which (to me at least) is somewhat mystifying, since it shows him sitting in a model T bathtub with autumn leaves falling on his hair. But both look satisfied and feel the gifts are a fair exchange. We drink Martinis on it. Like a summoned genie, a face appears at the kitchen door: Matt Barker. As we insist he have a Martini, his face lights like an eastern star. But Rosalie is waiting in the car. We urge her in, blushing and protesting. Now after a few rounds of drinks, the turkey is ready to come out of the oven, so everyone may as well stay on and more plates are added to the long table. . . .

This is Christmas in the country today.

Sugar Plums

Grind up some dried fruits—apricots, peaches, figs, pears, apples, prunes—along with some walnuts or filberts and some lemon peel, fresh or candied. Moisten part of the mixture with dark rum and the remainder with fine brandy, enough to bind all the ingredients together. Shape into small plums and roll in granulated sugar several times, repeating as the plums absorb the sugar. They will keep best in the refrigerator and mellow with time. Don't give this confection to young children no matter what they've read in fairy tales.

Good Things to Eat
by Laura Ingalls Wilder

Ma was busy all day long, cooking good things for Christmas. She baked salt-rising bread and rye'n'Injun bread, and Swedish crackers, and a huge pan of baked beans, with salt pork and molasses. She baked vinegar pies and dried-apple pies, and filled a big jar with cookies, and she let Laura and Mary lick the cake spoon.

One morning she boiled molasses and sugar together until they made a thick syrup, and Pa brought in two pans of clean, white snow from outdoors. Laura and Mary each had a pan, and Pa and Ma showed them how to pour the dark syrup in little streams on to the snow.

They made circles, and curlicues, and squiggledy things, and these hardened at once and were candy. Laura and Mary might eat one piece each, but the rest was saved for Christmas Day.

Divinity

2 c. sugar
1/2 c. light corn syrup
1/2 c. water
desh of salt

2 egg whites
1 tsp. vanilla
1 tsp. confectioners' sugar
1 c. chopped nuts
(1 c. crushed peppermint candy)

Mix sugar, corn syrup, water and salt in a heavy saucepan. Slowly bring to a boil, stirring until sugar is dissolved. Cook to hard-ball stage (260° on candy thermometer). While helper is stirring corn syrup mixture, cook should beat egg whites in a large bowl until they just hold their shape. When syrup is ready, pour slowly over egg whites in a steady thin stream, whipping slowly at the same time. Do not scrape pan. Beat until candy holds its shape, adding vanilla and confectioners' sugar. Add a cup of chopped nuts or as a variation, a cup of crushed peppermints just before ready to drop by teaspoonsful onto waxed paper. Let stand several hours until firm. Store in airtight container.

Family Festal Days
by Ethel Sabin Smith

Family festivals on the farm were the most memorable social events in our lives. High among them in joyousness was Father's annual oyster supper. Father felt that oysters were the most ambrosial food known to man, and that no one could really get his fill of them. Accordingly, during the first cold snap between Thanksgiving and Christmas, Father drove to Madison to get oysters, which he knew Mr. Piper, the best grocer in town, had shipped to him in barrels from the East. It was an all-day trip, even with the fast team on the light bobsled, because there was always other shopping to be done. Mother started to make a list weeks before, in anticipation of oyster day.

Our dinner table, at its greatest length, was not long enough for all the guests who came to the oyster supper, so the heavy pine kitchen table was brought in and set at right angles to the dining table. When it was covered with Mother's second-best long white cloth, it too looked festive. Of course our four grandparents were there, and Aunt Alice and Uncle Jim, and anyone who happened to be visiting at Grandfather's farm—and there was almost always some company there—and Aunt Anna and Uncle Frank with Arthur and Flossie and their small brother Carroll, younger than Ruth but older than my brother Herbert.

Father planned the supper and supervised the making of the stew to be certain it had plenty of oysters and lots of cream. That was followed by scalloped oysters with thick slices of home-cured bacon, sizzling and crisp, on top. There was celery and a bowl of the small sweet cucumber pickles which Mother made; and of course, hot rolls, and coffee for the grown-ups. In the center of each table were bowls of Wealthy apples for dessert, if anyone wanted dessert after perhaps two bowls of the stew and two helpings of scalloped oysters. Even if one did not really need an apple, it was difficult to resist a Wealthy, for to cut into one is like opening a treasure. The apple keeps the delicate pink of the bud in the perfumed flesh of the blow-end. Later, in the sitting room, we had some of Mother's butterscotch caramels and pop-corn balls, which Ruth and I had helped her make. Year after year, there was the same anticipation, the same menu, the same family faces, the same happiness.

Christmas was usually celebrated at Grandfather Sabin's farm and was indeed a gala day, because my Aunt Ella and Aunt Kate came home. Aunt Kate, Father's youngest and merriest sister, was still a student a the University at the time of one of the Christmas days I recall most vividly. Five of her particular University friends, three young men and two young women, had driven from Madison to share our midday Christmas dinner. They brought with them gales of laughter and good-natured pranks to play on "Katie's" solemn young nieces, to whom they seemed super-beings.

Aunt Ella was Father's older sister, who had won recognition in the field of education, and my attitude toward her was a complex of awe and affection. She brought a rich dignity to any occasion. Her wit was quick. Where she was, conversation moved at an accelerated pace and ranged over a wealth of topics, and she drew everyone into her electric circle of interest. At the Christmas dinner table Ruth, seated on the family Bible, and I, on the dictionary, sat silent and amazed at the good times grown-ups had together. How they could laugh! Sometimes, I thought the noise was going to make Herbert, in his high chair, cry. There was everything for dinner: both a roast goose and a baked him, and all the vegetables and pickles and jellies that go with them, and pies and nuts and candies.

After dinner we went from the dining-room into the sitting-room to wait there until Uncle Jim opened the double doors into the parlor, where the tree was. It took him some time to light all the candles, but everyone was burning brightly when at last we went in, and the parlor smelled of evergreen. There were presents for everyone. I liked mine pretty well, except that in one small oblong box from Aunt Alice, that I thought was going to have a string of coral beads, I found a scrubbing brush with stiff bristles: "To scrub your knees clean, Ethel, with love." I had carefully told Aunt Alice, before Christmas, that I hoped someone would give me coral beads to go with my new red cashmere dress.

After the present giving, Aunt Kate's friends left for the long drive to Madison and took some of the gaiety of the day with them. Aunt Alice hurried to make everything neat again, and then Grandmother said: "Now Ella, what have you brought to read aloud this year?" We made a circle around Aunt Ella. Father held Herbert in his arms and Ruth and I sat on the floor. She leaned against Mother and I leaned against Aunt Alice. The title of the Christmas story and its author escape me, but I recall that it had some dialect in it, which Aunt Ella handled expertly, and that she held us spellbound between laughter and tears for an hour or more. Grandmother sat in a low rocking chair beside Aunt Ella, and it was at Grandmother that Aunt Ella usually glanced when she looked up from her book. I saw their smiles go back and forth.

Then Christmas Day was over at last. Mother started to bundle us children into bonnets and coats and leggings, while Father hitched Jessie and Mollie to the light bobsled, ready for the four-mile drive back to our farm. We three children, my little brother sound asleep, and Ruth and I wide-eyed and still excited by the day, were tucked in between two buffalo robes on the floor of the sleigh. One was spread on the straw in the bottom and we lay upon it, and the other covered us up to our chins. Mother rode with Father on the spring seat, with another robe tucked around them and their collars turned up. Grandfather had come out in the cold to see us off and, though he was wrapped up, he kept jumping from one foot to the other not to get cold. Just as we were starting, Grandfather said: "Look! Northern Lights," as a pulse of vibrant light ebbed over the northern sky and even up to the zenith, where the stars sparkled clear and close.

The horses' feet made a muffled sound as they jogged down the driveway, because the snow wasn't hard-packed yet, but it was firm enough so you could hear the runners cutting into it. We did not have sleigh bells because Father said bells bothered Jessie. She always turned her ears back and twitched them when she heard bells. So the sound of our going was a quiet, smooth sound, so unlike the turning sound of wheels, and so eloquent of Christmas.

Christmas on Main Street

Christmas Greeting

This is fair greeting to my friends,
To those who come and those who go,
From one who to your linen lends
The whiteness of the driven snow.

Greeting to the ones who find
Their chiefest joy in linen fair,
Smooth as a grape's rich bloom outlined,
And laundered with the best of care.

And when my wagon standing waits
Beside the homes that know me best,
Greeting to those who ope the gates,
On north or south or east or west.

Fair greeting then with cheerful voice,
Long life and mirth and music's cheer,
And may my work your hearts rejoice
All through the onward coming year.

And as these pictures you admire,
And while these lines you lightly scan
Remember at the Christmas fire
This greeting from your laundryman.

Alford Brothers Steam Laundry, Madison, 1892

Hanging Our Stockings

by Gertrude Schroeder

The first thrill of Christmas was St. Nicholas Eve when we hung our long stockings at the foot of the bed. It was supposed to be only for one night, but we kids would hang the stockings for several nights and find candy, nuts and fruit in them. One time, my Dad got tired of filling them and put a potato in each one. That ended the St. Nick celebrations.

The Christmas presents were mostly clothes and games like Lotto, Parcheesi, Old Maid cards, marble games and the like. One year my brother Adlai got a rocking horse that is now at the Ozaukee County Historical Society's Pioneer Village.

One Christmas I got a doll with real hair donated by an aunt who had long brown hair. The doll's eyes opened and closed and had long dark lashes. I cherished it for years.

Sometimes father would put his hand into his coat pocket and pull out a piece of jewelry purchased at Armbruster's, whose store was then across from our home. The site is now the parking lot near the bakery. I remember getting a lavaliere with a diamond chip and another time, a ring with four amethysts, my birthstone. I wish I'd taken care of them. I got a stick pin from my godfather Henry Boerner which I'd wear, take off and put anywhere until my mother was tired of picking it up. She put it away and forgot where she put it. We never found it.

Cedarburg

Victorian Christmas

We had such a Christmas celebration. A jolly breakfast and a dinner with the table in beautiful violet, and wax candles for lights. Roast beef and plum pudding decked with holly and alight with brandy . . . and in the evening, the tree.

It was in the library and was so big it touched the ceiling. It was fixed on a crank thing and turned around and was full of lights and cotton snow and tinsel frost and adornments of all kinds, that are religiously saved and added to, from year to year, so that one heart shaped ginger cake some one showed me had appeared on every Christmas for twelve years.

Piled around it on the floor were presents too heavy to be hung from the branches. We were ushered in by music. . . . Santa Claus rushed in at the right moment and made a funny speech and commenced to distribute gifts by calling names as he cut the strings that caught the bundles to the tree.

. . . we all kept a quick eye on the swaying branches, with wet sponges on long wands ready to put out the high candles or any twigs that might ignite. The names were called so fast that the children were kept constantly on the jump. Some bundles were opened at once and jumping jacks, horns, and whistles were in active use; but most of us had chairs, or corners of shelves or a section of the piano for our piles that grew larger and larger, full of intoxicating suggestion as the distribution progressed.

West Superior, 1895

Making Mincemeat
by Elda Schweisser

Before the turn of the century, I remember the first sign that Christmas was getting near, was the night we had bowls of beef broth and crackers for supper. It never happened at any other time of the year. The reason was that my mother had bought a piece of beef, and had it simmering on the back of the coal-burning living room stove all day. It was seasoned with salt and papper, but no onions because of the beef's ultimate destiny.

This was the foundation for the holiday mincemeat. Next day came the chopping, not grinding; there was no meat grinder. Each kind of ingredient was put into the big, old, wooden chopping bowl and attacked with the steel chopping knife, until it was reduced to fine pieces. As my mother chopped the meat and apples and raisins, I always asked to help. But small arms were soon tired, and always glad to relinquish the job to her. Mother added spices, sugar, molasses, jelly, cider, raisins and currants.

All that day the wonderful smells sifted through the house. By evening, after many stirrings and tastings, the whole kettleful was transferred to a big stone crock, then covered and set in the "cold pantry" to ripen the flavors for the holidays.

New Glarus

New Glarus, Monroe and the surrounding areas in south central Wisconsin were settled in the early days of the territory by Swiss immigrants from the canton of Glarus. Their continuing pride in their heritage is shown by several summer festivals which feature authentic costumes, food, and music. It goes without saying that Christmas is a holiday kept in homes and hearts in a traditional way. Here are two Christmas recipes, one for a bread figure shaped like a gingerbread man, the other a fruit-filled cookie.

Grattimänner

2 c. lukewarm milk	2 Tbsp. shortening
2 Tbsp. honey (or sugar)	2 Tbsp. butter or margarine
1 Tbsp. salt	1 Tbsp. grated orange peel
1 cake fresh yeast (or 2 pkg. dried yeast)	

Glaze: 1 egg, beaten with fork
1 tsp. milk
pinch of salt

In small bowl dissolve yeast and honey in 1/2 c. lukewarm milk. Set aside until bubbly, about 10 minutes in a warm place. Meanwhile in a large bowl mix the flour, salt, and grated peel. When yeast mixture is ready, add it and remaining milk to the flour mixture, blending well. Let rest for 10 minutes. Add shortening and butter. Turn out onto floured surface and knead well, adding small amounts of flour if dough is too sticky. Be conservative with the flour as too much will make a stiff dry bread. It should be soft and pliable. Place bread in a large greased bowl, cover with a damp cloth, and leave in a warm place to rise until double in bulk, 1 to 2 hours. Turn dough out on a lightly floured surface and punch down until air bubbles are gone. Roll out a portion of the dough until flat, about 1/2 inch thick. Place a cookie cutter shape of a person over dough and cut around it with a knife or shape your own with knife or scissors. Place on baking sheet, leaving 2 inches between figures. Remember they will double in bulk.

Cover Grattimanner with towel and let rise as before for about 40 minutes. Brush each figure with glaze and decorate with almonds and raisins for eyes, etc. Leave uncovered for 20 minutes then brush with glaze again.

Bake in preheated 350° oven for 35 minutes, turning after 10 minutes for even browning. Grattimanner are done when glossy browny crust is firm. Cool on wire rack.

Glarner Zwetschge Tasche
(Glarus Prune Pockets)

1/3 c. sugar	1 egg
1/3 c. shortening	1 tsp. vanilla
2/3 c. honey	2-3/4 c. flour
	1 tsp. each salt and soda

Mix first 5 ingredients well then add dry ingredients. Mix well and chill for one hour. Divide dough into 3 parts, keeping unused portions refrigerated. Roll out one portion of dough on a slightly floured surface. Cut with large round cookie cutter into circles.

Place a tablespoon of fruit filling (prune filling: cooked mashed pitted prunes sweetened with honey) onto center of cookie. Fold dough over, forming half circle; seal edges. Bake 8 minutes in a preheated 350° oven. Glaze if desired with an egg yolk mixed with a teaspoon of water brushed on before baking.

The Promise of Opportunity

Mineral Point, founded in 1827, is one of the oldest cities in Wisconsin. Deposits of lead and zinc attracted Cornish miners to the area. While their life expectancy, forty-seven years, was not greatly changed in the Wisconsin mines, the promise of greater opportunities for their children encouraged them to stay. With them they brought the Cornish Pasty, a delicious meal-in-one consisting of potatoes, onions, and beef baked in a fold of pastry. The following is an authentic recipe used by the women of the First United Methodist Church, Mineral Point, for their annual fundraisers.

Cornish Pasty

Pasty crust:

4 c. flour
2 tsp. salt
1-1/2 c. lard (or shortening)

3/4 c. plus 2 Tbsp. cold water
2 eggs

Sift flour and salt together. Work in lard. Beat eggs slightly; add to cold water. Add to flour mixture; stir just to hold together. Divide into 6 parts. Roll out to about an 8 inch circle.

Pasty filling:

2 lbs. round steak (cubed)
3 c. potatoes (thinly sliced)
6 Tbsp. chopped onion

salt, pepper
1/2 c. ground suet
1 c. rutabagas, chopped

For each pasty combine 1/2 c. meat, 3/4 c. potatoes, 2 table-spoons chopped onion, 1/4 tsp. salt, 1/4 tsp. pepper, 1 Tbsp. suet, 1 Tbsp. rutabaga. Place on crust and moisten edge. Fold top half over and seal edge tightly so no juice leaks out. Put several holes on top with knife to allow steam to escape. Bake 1 hr. 20 min. in 325° oven.

* * * * *

This is a mouth-watering recipe for a real Cornish pasty in the real "Cousin Jack" (which is the dialogue):

"Go's on, my dear boy, w'at does thee knaw 'bout pasties? Thee's the kind of man w'at cut'n 'cross the middle and lets all that pretty juice run about over the plate. Thee's the kind of man w'at takes 'n right h'out of h'oven and gulps 'n daoen. Did thees ever 'ear of 'wrappin' a pasty? Duss thee knaw w'at 'appens then? Well, you take 'n aout of the h'oven with lovin' care. Thees wrap'n up careful in a great cloth and let 'n stand h'idle for a 'alf hour. There's things goin' on inside that pasty durin' that 'alf hour. The juice rolls around inside of 'n. It swishes up through the bits of turmit on the top. It boils up into the under side of the lovely crust, and then runs back faoen again, to atart'n all over. Then unwrap'n. Pick'n up in both 'ands. Start from the top and work daown. Tidd'n nawthin to 'oller 'about until you 'bout 'alfway or moor. Then you run smack into 'n. That dear old graavy is layin' there, restin, comfortable in its bed of taties, honions, mate and turmit. Thees waitin' there to run all over your great face, behind your ears and in your 'air—if you got any. You slohh on daown into 'n. Ee gets thicker'n thicker with every bite. Ee runs daown your shirt. "Ees 'ot, meaty and pretty-right daown to the last drop. And that, my son, is eatin' a great pasty as 'e should be et. So it's turmit, tatie, or lickey pasty. Wich will 'ee 'ave—?"

First United Methodist Church Cookbook, Mineral Point

✳ ✳ ✳ ✳ ✳

Now all our neighbors' chimneys smoke,
And Christmas logs are burning;
Their ovens with baked meats do choke,
And all their spits are turning.
Without the door let sorrow lie,
And if for cold it hap to die,
We'll bury it in Christmas pie,
And evermore be merry!

An American Club Christmas

The American Club, commissioned by Walter J. Kohler, was built to house unmarried immigrant workers, "single men of modest means" who came to work for the Kohler Company. They received a room, board, laundry service and encouragement to join special evening classes in English and citizenship sponsored by the Company. Opened in 1918 the American Club functioned for decades; in 1978 it was closed, then refurbished, and reopened as a resort and conference center. The basic structure, placed on the National Register of Historic Places, remains the same. Guests are invited, as residents were of old, to celebrate Christmas with "joyous and wholehearted spirit."

The American Club celebrated its first Christmas with the joyous and whole-hearted spirit for which it is already becoming noted. The festival began Saturday, December 21st, at the dinner hour.

The dining room had been beautifully decorated by a committee of the club people, assisted and directed by Miss Evangeline Kohler. Garlands of pine, cedar and holly festooned every available place, and beautiful wreaths of green graced the Honor Roll, walls and windows. Two artistically lettered legends conveyed the appropriate sentiments of the season. The spirit of Christmas seemed to emanate from a graceful Christmas tree, festooned, decorated and illuminated. Candles burned on all the tables. Finally American flags all about the room stirred patriotic minds to reflect that Old Glory typified at this season, in a peculiar way, the return of Peace and Good Will to the earth.

Ten members of the Kohler Band played Christmas hymns and carols and patriotic music. Mr. Carl Strassburger, of Sheboygan, played an appropriate selection on the violin.

Meanwhile, a good dinner was served and good cigars were passed around to the men.

At the close of the dinner, Mr. Walter J. Kohler read a cablegram from Capt. Herbert V. Kohler: "Merry Christmas to you all. All's well." Three cheers and a tiger were given for the men in the service. Mr. Kohler then thanked the men in the name of the Kohler Co., for their efficiency and willingness in the important work done here toward winning the war. The Star Spangled Banner was then played, everybody standing.

Christmas 1919, brought the usual festivities among us.

The members of the organization all received from the company a Christmas remembrance, the married men receiving a goose and the single men a pocket knife.

One novel Christmas observance was the lighting of a number of the little trees in front of the Club by means of small electric lights.

The real Christmas, of course, would take us into the homes of hundreds of people where good cheer and good will marked the observance of the day. The annual recurrence of the holiday finds it still new and welcome. Its spirit is one of which normal people will never tire; a spirit that, if it could be spread out over the year, rather than confined to one day, would doubtless be of unimaginable value.

Kohler News, Kohler

* * * * *

Perhaps some St. Clara girls have forgotten a holiday custom of their Alma Mater. Following a cherished tradition, every Christmas Eve she places in the window of the bay-window room high up near the Chapel, three lighted candles. Their cheerful glow can be seen for some distance in the encircling darkness outside, and while it lights the coming of the homeless Christ Child, it also typifies her warm affection for her widely-scattered children. For one bright beacon burns for all at St. Clara, a second for the Sisters on the missions, and a third for the Alumnae. May the peace and joy of a truly merry Christmas presage for them a happy and blessed New Year about to dawn.

St. Clara's Academy, Sinsinawa, 1924

Christmas in the Lutefisk Ghetto
by Art Lee

The most thrilling night of the year for us children was Christmas Eve. Much preparation was necessary for this night, notably the baking of Fattigman, Berliner, Sandbakkels, and Krumkake. Big loaves of julebrod were in the pantry, flanked by piles of lefse and flatbrod, and the barrel of apples was opened. The chores were done earlier and quicker, but the horses got an extra helping of oats, the cows more feed, the hogs a few more ears of corn, and the chickens several additional handfuls of their favorite grain mixture. Even the cats bulged from their extra supply of fresh warm milk. Finally the family meal, starting with the line of the mother. "Ver saa god." (Time to eat) and then the singing of "I denne sote Juletid," followed by the tale prayer, "I Jesu navn . . ." Then came the culinary parade: the lutefisk with rendered, hot melted butter, the spareribs, the rice pudding, the cranberry sauce, the tyteber, and all. Finally, at last, as far as the children are concerned, the meal is finished. Thanks is returned to the Heavenly Father, each one shakes hands with all the others and says "Takk for maten." (Thanks for the food.) Then all, except for the father, help clear the table and wash the dishes in near record time. Meanwhile the father has been in the mysterious closed off parlor and lighted the candles on the Christmas Tree. All gather before the closed door, the littlest ones first, almost breathless with eagerness. Then father opens the door! Such Oh's and Ah's and the beaming joy and sparkling eyes greet the lovely sight. After the tree has been admired for a few minutes, the father extinguishes the dangerously burning candles on the tree. Then it's time for the program, so all sing the standard songs, "Glade Jul," (Happy Christmas), "Her kommer dine arme smaa," (Here Comes Your Small Army) and other favorites. Children stand up in front of the tree and recite what parts they've had in the school Christmas program, and finally the program climaxes with father reading the Christmas Gospel story from St. Luke. Afterwards, all sit quietly, some obviously impatient, and then father finally tells the younger ones that it's now time to distribute the presents lying under the tree. That is the moment most waited for! A happy hubbub follows—comparing presents, thanking each other, trying out new toys, paging through new books, passing apples and candy, cracking nuts. Much laughter and merriment. Suddenly the clock strikes ten. That means bedtime as all are to be up early the next morning for Christmas services. The great evening has ended; the candles on the tables have flickered out, the last *god nat* (good night) said, the childrens' final prayers murmured, the last kerosene lamp quenched, and the peaceful quiet of Christmas Eve enfolds all, holding in its darkened hush the echoes of the song, "Silent Night, Holy Night."

Art Lee is a professor of history at Bemidji State University. Author of a number of books he has recorded the folkways of his own rural background in post World War II Wisconsin in The Lutefisk Ghetto *and* Leftover Lefse.

An Orange in One's Stocking

The things I remember are not unusual. Mother strung a long rope across the living room, on which we all hung our stockings. We had a Christmas tree also. We were sent upstairs early, but went down quietly on the stairs and tried to peep at them as they put up the presents.

Next morning an orange in one's stocking, along with candy and popcorn, was the greatest treat. For with no fruit stores as we now have them, oranges were to be found in the stores only at Christmastime. An orange for Christmas! That was something to remember and feel proud of having received! It was something worth telling to your playmates.

Christmas Eve services were held in the old Methodist church, and when we were older we were allowed to go along. I recall that inside the edifice were two long stoves—one on each side—filled with burning cordwood, from which ran stovepipes the full length of the church. Suspended by wires from the ceiling under the stovepipe joints were quart tin pails to catch the liquid soot that dripped. Light thrown into the church by silvered reflectors fastened to the wall behind the kerosene lamps gave all the light that was needed.

At the front of the church stood a large candlelighted Christmas tree for the Sunday School, but it was loaded with presents for the grownups as well. When the program carols had been sung the presents were distributed. Popcorn and candy were given out to the congregation, and the older children scrambled to capture the loops of popcorn and apples that decorated the tree. In those days everybody came to the church festivities in horse-drawn bobsleighs. With straw in the bottom of the sleigh box, soapstones at our feet, and covered with buffalo robes, we were kept warm for the ride. During the exercises the horses were heavily blanketed; at the end they were frisky as they sensed the imminence of the trip back to the farm barn.

Baraboo c. 1875

Circus Christmas

Now when I was growing up, Baraboo was a true circus city. The Barnum show wintered at Bridgeport, where it always had, but Ringling Brothers still had its winter quarters in Baraboo. They were an elaborate establishment that ran along both sides of the street beside the Baraboo River. There were many long brick animal barns and stables, a wardrobe building, electrical department, machine shop, wagon shop, blacksmith's shop, where the broad iron tires for the wagon wheels were forged and the horses shod. At this time the circus agents claimed that the show had 1002 horses. I am not sure, for I did not count them.

In addition, there were always about twenty-five or more wild animals in the menagerie—seven or eight lions, half a dozen tigers, a white leopard, two or three giraffes, a couple of hippos, llamas, zebras, monkeys, and a great many camels, which were used in the spectacles and parades.

Having achieved one ambition by masterminding Ringling Brothers' purchase of Barnum & Bailey, John Ringling was just starting to build the great financial empire which made him, for a time, one of the richest men in the world. But even he always returned to Baraboo for Christmas, and for the brotherly conclaves in which the affairs of the circus and of everything else pertaining to the family were decided. As long as his father and mother lived, Uncle John always came home for Christmas. Only once, in 1907, he did not quite make it.

When my grandmother heard that her son was unable to reach Baraboo until mid-January, she simply postponed Christmas. In this connection, we have a check for fifty dollars drawn to her order by Otto Ringling and dated December 24, 1907. She even refused to cash it until John came home. The check was never cashed.

Grandmother decreed that Christmas should fall on January 16, 1908. That evening all seven of her surviving children, their wives and offspring gathered as always in her home. My brother John was there; I was not yet born. As always, they had a roaring wonderful reunion with plenty of rousing arguments and homeric gustatory exploits. That night my grandmother died in her sleep. One may be sure she was very happy.

Henry Ringling North, *The Circus Kings*

To Springvale For Christmas
by Zona Gale

When President Arthur Tilton of Briarcliff College, who usually used a two-cent stamp, said, "Get me Chicago, please," his secretary was impressed, looked for vast educational problems to be in the making, and heard instead:

"Ed? Well, Ed, you and Rick and Grace and I are going out to Springvale for Christmas. . . . Yes, well, I've got a family too, you recall. But Mother was seventy last fall and—Do you realize that it's eleven years since we all spent Christmas with her? Grace has been every year. She's going this year. And so are we! And take her the best Christmas she ever had, too. Ed, Mother was *seventy* last fall. . . ."

At dinner, he asked his wife what would be a suitable gift, a very special gift, for a woman of seventy. And she said: "Oh, your mother. Well, dear, I should think the material for a good wool dress would be right. I'll select it for you, if you like. . . ." He said that he would see, and he did not reopen the subject.

In town on December twenty-fourth he timed his arrival to allow him an hour in a shop. There he bought a silver-gray silk of a fineness and a lightness which pleased him and at a price which made him comfortably guilty. And at the shop, Ed, who was Edward McKillop Tilton, head of a law firm, picked him up.

"Where's your present?" Arthur demanded.

Edward drew a case from his pocket and showed him a tiny gold wristwatch of decent manufacture and explained: "I expect you'll think I'm a fool, but you know that Mother has told time for fifty years by the kitchen clock, or else the shield of the black marble parlor angel who never goes—you get the idea?—and so I bought her this."

At the station was Grace, and the boy who bore her bag bore also a parcel of great dimensions.

"Mother already has a feather bed," Arthur reminded her.

"They won't let you take an automobile into the coach," Edward warned her.

"It's a rug for the parlor," Grace told them. "You know it is a parlor—one of the few left in the Mississippi Valley. And Mother has had that ingrain down since before we left home. . . ."

Grace's eyes were misted. Why would women always do that? This was no occasion for sentiment. This was a merry Christmas.

"Very nice. And Ricky'd better look sharp," said Edward dryly.

Ricky never did look sharp. About trains he was conspicuously ignorant. He had no occupation. Some said that he "wrote," but no one had ever seen anything that he had written. He lived in town— no one knew how—never accepted a cent from his brothers and was beloved of everyone, most of all of his mother.

"Ricky won't bring anything, of course," they said.

But when the train pulled out without him, observably, a porter came staggering through the cars carrying two great suit-cases and following a perturbed man of forty-something who said, "Oh, here you are!" as if it were they who were missing, and squeezed himself and his suitcases among brothers and sister and rug. "I had only a minute to spare," he said regretfully. "If I'd had two, I could have snatched some flowers. I flung 'em my card and told 'em to send 'em."

"Why are you taking so many lugs?" they wanted to know.

Ricky focused on the suitcases, "Just necessities," he said. "Just the presents. I didn't have room to get in anything else."

"Presents! What?"

"Well," said Ricky, "I'm taking books. I know Mother doesn't care much for books, but the bookstore's the only place I can get trusted."

They turned over his books: fiction, travels, biography, a new illustrated edition of the Bible—they were willing to admire his selection. And Grace said confusedly but appreciatively: "You know, the parlor bookcase has never had a thing in it excepting a green curtain over it!"

And they were all borne forward, well pleased.

Springvale has eight hundred inhabitants. As they drove through the principal street at six o'clock on that evening of De-cember twenty-fourth, all that they expected to see abroad was the popcorn wagon and a cat or two. Instead they counted seven automobiles and estimated thirty souls, and no one paid the slightest attention to them as strangers. Springvale was becoming metro-politan. There was a new church on one corner and a store building bore the sign *Public Library*. Even the little hotel had a rubber plant in the window and a strip of cretonne overhead.

The three men believed themselves to be a surprise. But, mindful of the panic to be occasioned by four appetites precipitated into a Springvale menage, Grace had told. Therefore the parlor was lighted and heated, there was in the air of the passage an odor of brown gravy which, no butler's pantry ever having inhibited, seemed a permanent savory. By the happiest chance, Mrs. Tilton had not heard their arrival nor—the parlor angel being in her customary eclipse and the kitchen grandfather's clock wrong—had she begun to look for them. They slipped in, they followed Grace down the hall, they entered upon her in her gray gingham apron worn over her best blue serge, and they saw her first in profile, frosting a lemon pie. With some assistance from her, they all took her in their arms at once.

"Aren't you surprised?" cried Edward in amazement.

"I haven't got over being surprised," she said placidly, "since I first heard you were coming!"

She gazed at them tenderly, with flour on her chin, and then said: "There's something you won't like. We're going to have the family dinner tonight."

Their clamor that they would entirely like that did not change her look.

"Our church couldn't pay the minister this winter," she said, "on account of the new church building. So the minister and his wife are boarding around with the congregation. Tomorrow's their day to come here for a week. It's a hard life and I didn't have the heart to change 'em."

Her family covered their regret as best they could and entered upon her little feast. At the head of her table, with her four "children" about her, and Father's armchair left vacant, they perceived that she was not quite the figure they had been thinking her. In this interval they had grown to think of her as a pathetic figure. Not because their father had died, not because she insisted on Springvale as a residence, not because of her eyes. Just pathetic. Mothers of grown children, they might have given themselves the suggestion, were always pathetic. But here was Mother, a definite person, with poise and with ideas, who might be proud of her offspring, but who, in her heart, never forgot that they were her offspring and that she was the parent stock.

"I wouldn't eat two pieces of that pie," she said to President Tilton; "it's pretty rich." And he answered humbly: "Very well, Mother." And she took with composure Ricky's light chant:

"Now, you must remember, wherever you are,
That you are the jam, but your mother's the jar."

"Certainly, my children," she said. "And I'm about to tell you when you may have your Christmas presents. Not tonight. Christmas Eve is no proper time for presents. It's stealing a day outright! And you miss the fun of looking forward all night long. The only proper time for the presents is after breakfast on Christmas morning, after the dishes are washed. The minister and his wife may get here any time from nine on. That means we've got to get to bed early!"

President Arthur Tilton lay in his bed looking at the muslin curtain on which the streetlamp threw the shadow of a bare elm which he remembered. He thought: She's a pioneer spirit. She's the kind who used to go ahead anyway, even if they had missed the emigrant party, and who used to cross the plains alone. She's the backbone of the world. I wish I could megaphone that to the students at Briarcliff who think their mothers "try to boss," them!

"Don't leave your windows open too far," he heard from the hall. "The wind's changed."

In the light of a snowy morning the home parlor showed the cluttered commonplace of a room whose furniture and ornaments were not believed to be beautiful and most of them known not to be useful. Yet when—after the dishes were washed—these five came to the leather chair which bore the gifts, the moment was intensely satisfactory. This in spite of the sense of haste with which the parcels were attacked—less the minister and his wife arrive in their midst.

"That's one reason," Mrs. Tilton said, "why I want to leave part of my Christmas for you until I take you to the train tonight. Do you care?"

"I'll leave a present I know about until then too," said Ricky. "May I?"

"Come on now, though," said President Arthur Tilton. "I want to see Mother get her dolls."

It was well that they were not of an age to look for exclamations of delight from Mother. To every gift her reaction was one of startled rebuke.

"Grace! How could you? All that money! Oh, it's beautiful! But the old one would have done me all my life. . . . Why, Edward! You extravagant boy! I never had a watch in my life. You ought not to have gone to all that expense. Arthur Tilton! A silk dress! What a firm piece of goods! I don't know what to say to you—you're all too good to me!"

At Ricky's books she stared and said: "My dear boy, you've been very reckless. Here are more books than I can ever read—now. Why, that's almost more than they've got to start the new library with. And you spent all that money on me!"

It dampened their complacence, but they understood her concealed delight and they forgave her an honest regret of their modest prodigality. For, when they opened her gifts for them, they felt the same reluctance to take the hours and hours of patient knitting for which these stood.

"Hush, and hurry," was her comment, "or the minister'll get us!"

The minister and his wife, however, were late. The second side of the turkey was ready and the mince pie hot when, toward noon, they came to the door—a faint little woman and a thin man with beautiful, exhausted eyes. They were both in some light glow of excitement and disregarded Mrs. Tilton's efforts to take their coats.

"No," said the minister's wife. "No. We do beg your pardon. But we find we have to go into the country this morning."

"It is absolutely necessary that we go into the country," said the minister earnestly. "This morning," he added impressively.

"Into the country! You're going to be here for dinner."

They were firm. They had to go into the country. They shook hands almost tenderly with these four guests. "We just heard about you in the post office," they said. "Merry Christmas—oh, merry Christmas! We'll be back about dark."

They left their two shabby suitcases on the hall floor and went away.

"All the clothes they've got between them would hardly fill these up," said Mrs. Tilton mournfully. "Why on earth do you suppose they'd turn their back on a dinner that smells so good and go off into the country at noon on Christmas Day? They wouldn't do that for another invitation. Likely somebody's sick," she ended, her puzzled look denying her tone of finality.

"Well, thank the Lord for the call to the country," said Ricky shamelessly. "It saved our day."

They had their Christmas dinner; they had their afternoon—safe and happy and uninterrupted. Five commonplace-looking folk in a commonplace-looking house, but the eye of love knew that this was not all. In the wide sea of their routine they had found and taken for their own this island day, unforgettable.

"I thought it was going to be a gay day," said Ricky at its close, "but it hasn't. It's been heavenly! Mother, shall we give them the rest of their presents now, you and I?"

"Not yet," she told them. "Ricky, I want to whisper to you."

She looked so guilty that they all laughed at her. Ricky was laughing when he came back from that brief privacy. He was still laughing mysteriously when his mother turned from a telephone call.

"What do you think?" she cried. "That was the woman that brought me my turkey. She knew the minister and his wife were to be with me today. She wants to know why they've been eating a lunch in a cutter out that way. Do you suppose . . ."

They all looked at one another doubtfully, then in abrupt conviction. "They went because they wanted us to have the day to ourselves!"

"Arthur," said Mrs. Tilton with immense determination, "let me whisper to you, too." And from that moment's privacy he also returned smiling, but a bit ruefully.

"Mother ought to be the president of a university," he said.

"Mother ought to be the head of a law firm," said Edward.

"Mother ought to write a book about herself," said Ricky.

"Mother's Mother," said Grace, "and that's enough. But you're all so mysterious, except me."

"Grace," said Mrs. Tilton, "you reminded me that I want to whisper to you."

Their train left in the late afternoon. Through the white streets they walked to the station, the somber little woman, the buoyant, capable daughter, the three big sons. She drew them to seclusion down by the baggage room and gave them four envelopes.

"Here's the rest of my Christmas for you," she said. "I'd rather you'd open it on the train. Now, Ricky, what's yours?"

She was firm to their protests. The train was whistling when Ricky owned up that the rest of his Christmas present for his mother was a brand-new daughter, to be acquired as soon as his new book was off the press. "We're going to marry on the advance royalty," he said importantly, "and live on . . ." The rest was lost in the roar of the express.

"Edward!" shouted Mrs. Tilton. "Come here. I want to whisper. . . ."

She was obliged to shout it, whatever it was. But Edward heard, and nodded, and kissed her. There was time for her to slip something in Ricky's pocket and for the other good-bys, and then the train drew out. From the other platform they saw her brave, calm face against the background of the little town. A mother of "grown children" pathetic? She seemed to them at that moment the one supremely triumphant figure in life.

They opened their envelopes soberly and sat soberly over the contents. The note, scribbled to Grace, explained: Mother wanted to divide up now what she had had for them in her will. She would keep one house and live on the rent from the other one, and "here's all the rest." They laughed at her postscript:

"Don't argue. I ought to give the most—I'm the mother."

"And look at her," said Edward solemnly. "As soon as she heard about Ricky, there at the station, she whispered to me that she wanted to send Ricky's sweetheart the watch I'd just given her. Took it off her wrist then and there."

"That must be what she slipped in my pocket," said Ricky.

It was.

"She asked me," he said, "if I minded if she gave those books to the new Springvale Public Library."

"She asked me," said Grace, "if I cared if she gave the new rug to the new church that can't pay its minister."

President Arthur Tilton shouted with laughter. "When we heard where the minister and his wife ate their Christmas dinner," he said, "she whispered to ask me whether she might give the silk dress to her when they get back tonight."

All this they knew by the time the train reached the crossing where they could look back on Springvale. On the slope of the hill lay the little cemetery, and Ricky said, "And she told me that if my flowers got there before dark, she'd take them up to the cemetery for Christmas for Father. By night she won't have even a flower left to tell her we've been there."

"Not even the second side of the turkey," said Grace, "and yet I think . . ."

"So do I," her brothers said.

Zona Gale wrote fiction, drama, poetry and criticism. Though a reporter for the Milwaukee Journal, then the New York Evening News she chronicled small town life, using her hometown, Portage, for inspiration. She received a Pulitzer Prize in 1921. Active in political and civic affairs, a pacifist and feminist, she supported La Follette's Progressives and served for years as an influential member of the Board of Regents of the University of Wisconsin.

Memories of a River City
by Edna Ferber

Pioneer families of many years before, coming upon a cool green oasis after heart-breaking days through parched desert and wind-swept plains, must have felt much as the Ferber family did as it arrived in Appleton, Wisconsin, and looked about at the smiling valley in whose arms the town so contentedly nestled. A lovely little town of sixteen thousand people; tree-shaded, prosperous, civilized. The Fox River ran through it, cool and swift and strong, a willing beast of burden, a benign giant whose power turned mill wheels, energized factories, created industry, brought prosperity. Its waterways hummed with huge paper mills fed by the forests of Michigan and Wisconsin. All about it lay small prosperous towns like itself—Kaukauna, Neenah, Menasha, Little Chute. Giant elms and oaks, arching overhead, made cool green naves of the summer streets. The townspeople owned their houses, tended their lawns and gardens. They were substantial, intelligent, progressive. They read, they traveled, they went to the theater, heard music, educated their children at the local college, a Methodist institution called Lawrence University, or sent them to Beloit College, or Notre Dame, or the University of Wisconsin at Madison. Appleton represented the American small town at its best. A sense of well-being pervaded it. It was curiously modern and free in the best sense of the woods. Cliques, malice, gossip, snobbishness—all the insular meannesses—were strangely lacking in this thriving community. Trouble, illness and death were to come upon us there in the next few years, but sympathy and friendship leavened them and made them bearable.

I was busy having fun. I played, I read, I went to school, I rode my bicycle. With Esther or Belle or Frances I scoured the near-by country woods for wildflowers and came home laden (we'd know better now) with delicate hepaticas, with miniature lilies called trillium, with violets, Dutchman's breeches, saucy little Johnny-jump-ups, mandrakes—and sunny clumps of cowslips. In the autumn these same woods yielded hickory nuts, black walnuts, thorn apples. We would crack the hard green nutshells between stones and pick out the half-ripe meats with fingers stained tabacco brown from the juices inside the shells. There were picnics along the lovely banks of the Fox; we watched the excursion boats going through the locks, a fascinating sight as they eerily sank, sank in the first lock, then rose majestically in the second.

In the winter there was superb skating on the river. From November until March or even April the streets and sidewalks were covered with snow and ice. The bottom layer, formed by the first snows, became a steel-like sheet, and to this were added layer on layer, so that by February you walked on a solid glacier. Sometimes the temperature would go down to eighteen below zero. No one dreamed of staying indoors because of this. The cold cut your forehead like a knife. Your walk was a little trot, skillfully balanced so as not to slip on the tricky ice. On Saturdays and after school we went bobsled-catching, roving the streets like a horde of young Tartars. A farmer would come along on his bobsled. Out we rushed and flipped its broad runners, hanging on the side of the box-body

as the horses plunged through the snow, our feet swishing against the roadway drifts, our mittened hands stiff with cold. You stayed on the bob until you espied another headed in the opposite direction. Then off you leaped and caught a ride home. I don't know why this was considered such a grand sport, but it was. Wisconsin spoiled me forever for one-season climates. Stinging cold white winters, hot golden summers, springtime brilliant as a sword thrust, autumns that were like a conflagration in every street and road and farm site—the seasons were not marked merely by December, April, July and September. They were spectacular events, varied and clearly defined as phenomena.

> *Edna Ferber's family lived in several midwestern states before settling in Appleton when she was eleven. At seventeen she started her professional writing career as a $3-a-week reporter for the* Appleton Crescent, *and later wrote for the Milwaukee* Journal. *She was the author of numerous short stories, plays, and best selling novels, such as So Big, Cimmaron, Giant, Showboat, a number of which were dramatized as plays or movies.*

The Way it Was in Milwaukee
by Emma Welke

The Christmas season in Milwaukee at the turn of the century was quite different from what it is now. Lighted candles were set into holders and then clipped to tree sprigs. Cookies in the shape of birds, bells and stars were bought from a bakery and were strung up or hung on the tree as decorations. There was no electricity in those days.

Our flower business prospered at this time of the year. Primroses and Jerusalem cherry plants were popular; poinsettia plants were rare. Around 1903 or 1904, we could get only two poinsettia plants during the entire holiday season. We sold them for $3 apiece. I remember my hands used to be bloody from working with holly and the wire frame which held the wreath together. Holly wreaths are now machine made.

* * * * *

In this city the custom of decorating a Christmas tree for the enjoyment of the little ones seems to be confined largely to the German element of the population, and the trade in trees during the past week on the South Side and in the Northwest part of the city is extensive. The sidewalk on Third Street above Chestnut resembles a miniature forest, the bushes being erected on every inch of spare space. . . . For fifty cents a very fair-sized Christmas tree can be secured and when it occupies the position of honor in the parlor, decked with its gay-colored trappings and bearing its load of toys and candies it becomes a beautiful object to the happy youngsters. The giant trees of California would be nothing in the estimation of the children when compared to this stunted little bush that bears happiness on every bough.

Milwaukee Sentinel, December 23, 1883

Christmas for a Dollar

First the tree, fifteen cents secures a splendid one. Somewhere in the shed or cellar is an old box, just the thing to set it in. Ten cents buys eight good candles that can be cut in two pieces. A pin stuck stoutly wherever a light is wanted, will hold the taper well in place. Five cents gets a pound of corn for popping. Then purchase twenty cents worth of stick candy with a quarter pound of raisins (five cents) to sprinkle with it. Gauze to make little bags in which the candy could hang on the tree takes another five cents. Now forty cents still remains, and with it can be purchased a whittling knife with two blades (fifteen cents) for a boy and a set of toy dishes (twenty cents) for a girl. The remaining nickle can be used to buy a brightly colored Christmas card, and the children's joy will be complete.

Milwaukee Sentinel, December 20, 1880

A German Christmas

by Mrs. Fritz Bauer

I would like to add my Christmas eve memories in those of Mrs. Emil Welke.

Our tree was also decorated with wax candles in holders that snapped onto branches. No electric lights can produce the majesty of such an old fashioned tree! We had heavy gold and silver balls, about three inches in diameter, that were hung on the lower branches to weight them down. How well I remember the candy cherries with a connecting wire to drape over the branches. Garlands of silver tinsel hung from branch to branch. Our ornaments were beautiful. They were from my grandfather's toy store. He had the first toy store here in Milwaukee.

When the children were ready and the tree was illuminated, we were called into the parlor. Then my mother sang "Stille Nacht, heilige Nacht" accompanied by my father on the piano. Both were very talented. Our gifts were piled high on the table at our respective places plus the intriguing "bunte Teller." That was an old time soup plate, which had a broad, flat rim. It was filled with the following: A large California orange in the center, almonds, hazel nuts, walnuts and Brazil nuts in the shell, surrounding the orange. Arranged neatly over this were hazel nut Lebkuchen, honey Lebkuchen, Pfaster steine, weisse und braune Pfeffernuesse, natural yellow butter cookies, old fashioned chocolate drops, miniature fruits and vegetables of marzipan, baked by the late Mr. Joseph H. Kopp, who made them so realistic that each was a work of art. Add to this glistening colored French creams and the climax for us children, a white or brown mouse of French cream with pink frosting eyes and snout and tail of brown twine. These you could buy only at William Steinmeyer at 3rd and Highland.

Pardon me for mentioning goodies in German. But when translated into English, the charm is lost.

Braune Pfeffernuesse

6 c. sifted flour	1/8 tsp. ground cardamon
2 tsp. baking powder	5 eggs
1/2 tsp. salt	2 c. light brown sugar
1/2 tsp. black pepper	firmly packed
1/2 tsp. mace	3 tablespoons black coffee
1/2 tsp. nutmeg	1 c. ground blanched almonds
1 tsp. cloves	1 tsp. grated lemon peel
1 tsp. allspice	4 oz. chopped citron
3 tsp. cinnamon	1/2 c. confectioners' sugar
1/4 tsp. ground anise	

Sift flour with baking powder, salt, pepper, and spices. Set aside. In a large mixer bowl beat eggs with electric mixer until fluffy, about 5 minutes. Gradually beat in brown sugar. Beat in flour mixture, a fourth at a time, adding a tablespoon of coffee, finishing with the flour. Fold in almonds, lemon peel, and citron. Cover dough and refrigerate until chilled, at least 2 hours. When dough is ready roll into balls, using a tablespoon of dough for each ball. Place on lightly greased cookie sheets. Bake in preheated 300° oven for 18 to 20 minutes, cool; then roll in confectioners' sugar. Store in tins; the flavor increases with age.

Weisse Pfeffernuesse

4 c. flour	3 c. sugar
1/2 c. shortening	4 eggs
rind of one lemon	2 1/2 tablespoons cinnamon

Mix flour and cinnamon together, set aside. Cream shortening, add sugar, then eggs one at a time beating well after each addition. Add grated lemon. Beat in flour mixture, mixing to smooth dough. Chill. When dough is ready, make into small balls, and place on lightly greased cookie sheet. Bake at 375° about 10 minutes. Frost with lemon glaze as soon as they come out of the oven.
Lemon glaze: mix a cup of powdered sugar with enough lemon juice (from above lemon) to make a thin, soupy glaze.

Wilia Supper

In the Polish homes of Milwaukee's South Side the Wilia Supper began the Christmas Eve celebration. The day before Christmas was by Church rule a fast day of light meals and no meat. Cooking and baking had however begun at an early hour for there were many traditional foods to be prepared for Wilia and also Christmas day dinner. The Wilia supper made up for the fasting, a seven to eleven course meal which although still meatless was fully rich fare: pickled herring and pickled mushrooms, clear beet soup, creamed soup, baked and fried fish, creamed fish soup with dumplings, saurkraut with legumes or mushrooms, pierogi, a dough cooked like a dumpling and filled with cheese or potatoes or mushrooms or saurkraut or fruit, rich pastries, poppy seed streusel, nuts, and candies. At midnight it was time for Pasterka or the Shepherds' Mass.

Poppy Seed Streusel

1 c. milk	1 tsp. salt
1/4 c. lukewarm water	4 egg yolks
2 yeast cakes	4 c. flour
1/4 c. butter	1 tsp. vanilla
1/2 c. sugar	1/2 tsp. almond

Dissolve yeast in lukewarm water and set aside. Scald milk and cool until lukewarm. Beat egg yolks with salt until thick. Cream butter with sugar. Add flavoring and egg yolks. Add yeast. Add sifted flour alternately with cooled milk beginning and ending with flour. Knead until dough leaves the fingers. Cover with a damp cloth and let rise again until doubled. On floured board divide dough in two. Roll each half into rectangular shape to thickness of finger. Spread with poppy seed filling. Roll up tightly like a jelly roll, beginning with wide side. Pinch together the edges to seal in filling. Place each on a greased pan 13 x 4 1/2 x 2 1/2 (cookie sheet may be substituted, let rise until double, decrease baking time by 1/3 and check for doneness). Cover and let rise until dough fills the pan. Bake 45 minutes in 350° oven.

Poppy Seed Filling

2 c. ground poppy seed	1 tsp. vanilla extract
1 1/2 c. milk	1/2 tsp. almond extract
1 c. sugar or 3/4 c. honey	1/2 c. golden raisins
2 eggs	

Scald milk and add poppy seed. Cook until milk is absorbed, stirring constantly (about 5 minutes). Add sugar and cook stirring another two minutes. Remove from heat. Beat eggs slightly; stir a little of the hot poppy mixture into the eggs. Then add eggs to poppy seeds, return to heat and stir until thick, but do not boil. Remove from heat, add flavorings and raisins. Use when cool. (Canned-poppy seed filling can be used.)

Keeping Christmas

by Dr. Henry Van Dyke

It is a good thing to observe Christmas Day. The mere marking of times and seasons, when men agree to stop work and make merry together, is a wise and wholesome custom. It reminds a man to set his own little watch, now and then, by the great clock of humanity, which runs on sun time.

But there is a better thing than the observance of Christmas Day, and that is, keeping Christmas.

Are you willing to forget what you have done for other people, and to remember what other people have done for you; to ignore what the world owes you, and to think what you owe the world; to see that your fellow-men are just as real as you are, and to try to look behind their faces to their hearts, hungry for joy; to own that probably the only good reason for your existence is not what you are going to get out of life, but what you are going to give to life; to close your book of complaints against the management of the universe, and look around you for a place where you can sow a few seeds of happiness—are you willing to do these things even for a day? Then you can keep Christmas.

Are you willing to stoop down and consider the needs and the desires of little children; to remember the weakness and loneliness of people who are growing old; to stop asking how much your friends love you, and ask yourself whether you love them enough; to bear in mind the things that other people have to bear on their hearts; to try to understand what those who live in the same house with you really want, without waiting for them to tell you; to make a grave for your ugly thoughts, and a garden for your kindly feelings, with the gate open—are you willing to do these things even for a day? Then you can keep Christmas.

Are you willing to believe that love is the strongest thing in the world—stronger than hate, stronger than evil, stronger than death—and that the blessed Life which began in Bethlehem nineteen hundred years ago is the image and brightness of the Eternal Love? Then you can keep Christmas.

And if you keep it for a day, why not always?

But you can never keep it alone.

Immanuel Presbyterian Church, Milwaukee, 1910

One Year Done, and One Begun
by August Derluth

A solitary rabbit track alone
companions man's across the light-misshapen wintered park,
ringed 'round by lightless houses in the dark
where each man has a world that is his own.

Standing in that wooded place,
where his own small mark crosses the smaller track,
a man knows that in any year's last hour, looking back,
the year gone by and that before are but a little space.

Pausing in the snow-held park to hear
the midnight bells ring out the year,
a man, passing time, can know how time passes him.

Already now Arcturus foretells spring low on the eastern rim.

New Year's Party

On Monday evening, January 2nd, Severance and Williams Band will give their annual New Year's Ball at Metropolitan Hall on which occasion there will be a full band of six pieces, and everything will be arranged to the entire satisfaction of those who take part in the proceedings. Of course we need not say a word to our townspeople concerning this matter for they are sure to be there; but to our friends from abroad—from Elkhorn, Delavan, Sugar Creek, LaGrange, Richmond, Lima, Johnstown, Palmyra, Eagle, Fort Atkinson, etc. we would say, if you want a nice time just come and join us in our New Year's Party, and we will guarantee you will not regret it. We shall expect you, anyhow.

Register, Whitehall, 1861

Swiss New Year
by Millard Tschudy

The Swiss of New Glarus, like those of Old Glarus, treated the passing of one year to another as an event of considerable magnitude and they had a singular routine for observing it. But their title for the event was different. They called it Old Year's Eve, on the theory that until midnight December 31, the Old Year was expiring. From midnight through all of Jan. 1 was the beginning of the New Year.

For years, Schweizers here looked forward to 11:30 p.m. Dec. 31, when church bells rang, accompanied by the tooting of whistles at the milk condensary, the brewery and the locomotive down by the depot. Shortly before midnight the serenade ended, only to begin with newed vigor at midnight, continuing for another half hour.

Families were gathered at tables loaded with nourishing, heavy pear bread, delightful, crumbly coffee cake, cookies, and heady homemade wines reserved for this night of nights. An essential luxury was fresh cream whipped stiff with hazelnut switches, eaten from a common giant bowl in the center of the sturdy table. Capricious diners lobbed spoons of whipped cream at each other until they looked like gardens of white mushrooms.

A knock on the door brought a group of masked revellers, possibly neighbors or dancers taking time off from an uptown schottische, or waltz, offering greetings in return for a bit of the grape, fresh goodies, and, hoping that the year had been good enough to produce a few coins.

The last hours of the year was the one time youngsters got to stay up with their elders. They sneaked bits of salt pork and whatever they could carry off to a corner by the chimney for nibbling while eavesdropping on oldsters reminiscing, making predictions of coming events or joining in favorite songs. Even Grandma took time off from her kitchen to recite a favorite childhood poem or story of her youth.

The first day of the new year had its own traditions. The first youngster up and around that morning won for himself the coveted title of "Stubefuchs," (parlor fox) denoting his agility at getting out of bed the morning after the big night. It was pronounced for the whole household to hear that the Stubefuchs would be prosperous and succeed through the year. The second one up was the Fischterschuebble (window pane) whose responsibility it was to inform the family who was passing by the house, who was turning in. Booby prize went to the last one up. He was named the Silvester and was the subject of practical jokes and sly remarks through the day, accused of being one day behind everyone else. One New Glarner, always a Stubefuchs and never a Silvester, admits now that he had his clothes ready all night, giving him an unbeatable head start over his brothers.

In New Glarus, youngsters still perambulatory after midnight greeted relatives and friends with "Ich bin ein kleiner knab, und wuensch dir was ich kann. Ich wuensch dir glueck und segen, und a langes leben, und a guets Nues Jahr." (I'm a little boy and wish you what I can. I wish you luck and blessings, and a long life, and a good New Year). The reward was often a shiny silver dollar.

This year, as in years past, the Swiss here will appropriately greet each other at the proper time with "E guets Nueues" (A good new one).

Monroe Evening Times, December 31, 1973

New Year, 1888

by Ella Wheeler Wilcox

As the old year sinks down in Time's ocean,
　　Stand ready to launch with the new,
And waste no regrets, no emotion,
　　As the masts and the spars pass from view.
Weep not if some treasures go under,
　　And sink in the rotten ship's hold,
That blithe bonny barque sailing yonder
　　May bring you more wealth than the old.

For the world is forever improving,
　　All the past is not worth one-to-day,
And whatever deserves our true loving,
　　Is stronger than death or decay.
Old love, was it wasted devotion?
　　Old friends, were they weak or untrue?
Well, let them sink there in mid ocean,
　　And gaily sail on to the new.

Throw overboard toil misdirected,
　　Throw overboard ill-advised hope,
With aims which, your soul has detected,
　　Have self as their centre and scope.
Throw overboard usless regretting
　　For deeds which you cannot undo,
And learn the great art of forgetting
　　Old things which embitter the new.

Sing who will of dead years departed,
　　I shroud them and bid them adieu,
And the song that I sing, happy-hearted,
　　Is a song of the glorious new.

A Sense of Place

by George F. Kennan

I came to Princeton directly from St. John's Military Academy (Delavan). The progression was not a usual one. I owed it partly to the excitement and sense of revelation derived from reading Scott Fitzgerald's *This Side of Paradise* in my senior year at school, and partly to the help and encouragement of the St. John's dean, the late Henry Holt, a modest, shrewd, and dedicated pedagogue.

I arrived in Princeton on a hot evening in September 1921. The taxi carried me up University Place and down Nassau Street—along two sides of the campus; and as I discerned, through its windows, the shapes of the Gothic structures around Holder Hall, my penchant for the creation of imaginative wonders reached some sort of a crescendo. Mystery and promise, glamour and romance seemed to glow, like plasma, from these dim architectural shapes.

The reality was of course different. I was the last student admitted. I knew not a soul in college or town. I was given the last furnished room in the most remote of those gloomy rooming houses far off campus to which, at that time, late-coming freshmen were relegated. I was a year younger than most members of my class, and even more immature in manner than this tender age would suggest. I was hopelessly and crudely Midwestern. I had no idea how to approach boys from the East. I could never find the casual tone. My behavior knew only two moods: awkward aloofness and bubbling enthusiasm.

Perhaps a bit of ill-fortune also played a part. Come Christmas of my freshman year, lacking the money to go home and fearing to burden my father if I asked him for it, I went to nearby Trenton and got a temporary job with the post office as a mail carrier. Bright and early on the first day of these labors I was given the usual leather sack, brimming with bundles of letters, and dispatched southward by trolley car to the slums of the city. The letters in the bundles, my supervisors assured me, were in perfect order; I had only to find the beginning street and the letters themselves would then guide me along my route.

Wet snow was falling this dark December day; an inch or two of it had already accummulated on the streets. Fumbling with the first of my bundles, I hopped off the car at the appointed stop. As I did so the bundle opened and broke; the letters spilled out partly on the rear platform of the car, partly onto the snow-covered street. Amid honking cars and clanging trolleys. I frantically gathered them up again and set forth on my rounds. But now they were in wild disorder; not even the streets, much less house numbers, followed in sequence. All day, I trudged desperately back and forth around those dreary, slush-covered thoroughfares, retracing my steps a dozen times, plaguing innumerable passersby with requests for directions, recoiling from the sights and smells that assailed me when people answered the doorbells. It was late evening before I disposed of my load; and I finished the day by eating my one meal—for fifty cents—in a squalid little restaurant somewhere along my beat.

So went the days before Christmas, not all as unhappy as this, but not dissimilar. By the afternoon of Christmas Day, the twenty-eight dollars then required for a day-coach passage to Milwaukee had been earned, and I went proudly home in this humble fashion. But somewhere along the line, whether in Trenton's slums or on the day coach, I had contracted scarlet fever.

The illness overtook me at home, suddenly and with violence, one ghastly afternoon around New Year's. There was great commotion in the family. This was long before the time of penicillin. The worst, not unreasonably, was feared. My sisters, sure that they had seen the last of me, were prematurely packed off, the same evening, to their respective colleges. I was relegated to the third floor of the house where, attended by a trained nurse, I remained in quarantine until Easter. When I returned to college, spring was upon us; the academic year was drawing to a close, coteries and friendships had already coagulated. To these tight and secure little communities there were now few paths of access, particularly to one who was younger than most of the others, behind in his studies, forbidden participation in sport, and too poor to share in the most common avocations.

I remained, therefore, an oddball on campus, not eccentric, nor ridiculed or disliked, just imperfectly visible to the naked eye.

In these circumstances, Princeton was for me not exactly the sort of experience reflected in *This Side of Paradise*. The portrayal in the hauntingly beautiful epilogue to *The Great Gatsby* of the Midwesterner's reaction to the fashionable East held, to be sure, such familiarity for me that when I first read it, while still in college, I went away and wept unmanly tears.

Holiday Epilogue, The Great Gatsby

by F. Scott Fitzgerald

One of my most vivid memories is of coming back West from prep school and later from college at Christmas time. Those who went farther than Chicago would gather in the old dim Union Station at six o'clock of a December evening, with a few Chicago friends, already caught up into their own holiday gayeties, to bid them a hasty good-by. I remember the fur coats of the girls returning from Miss This-or-That's and the chatter of frozen breath and the hands waving overhead as we caught sight of old acquaintances, and the matchings of invitations: "Are you going to the Ordways'? the Herseys'? the Schultzes'?" and the long green tickets clasped tight in our gloved hands. And last the murky yellow cars of the Chicago, Milwaukee & St. Paul railroad looking cheerful as Christmas itself on the tracks beside the gate.

When we pulled out into the winter night and the real snow, our snow, began to stretch out beside us and twinkle against the windows, and the dim lights of small Wisconsin stations moved by, a sharp wild brace came suddenly into the air. We drew in deep breaths of it as we walked back from dinner through the cold vestibules, unutterably aware of our identity with this country for one strange hour, before we melt indistinguishably into it again.

That's my Middle West—not the wheat or the prairies or the lost Swede towns, but the thrilling returning trains of my youth, and the street lamps and sleigh bells in the frosty dark and the shadows of holly wreaths thrown by lighted windows on the snow. I am part of that, a little solemn with the feel of those long winters, a little complacent from growing up in the Carraway house in a city where dwellings are still called through decades by a family's name. I see now that this has been a story of the West, after all—Tom and Gatsby, Daisy and Jordan and I, were all Westerners, and perhaps we possessed some deficiency in common which made us subtly unadaptable to Eastern life. . . .

* * * * *

O, world! O, life! O, hearts in sorrow sighing!
    Remember that to-day
Across the waste of time about you lying,
    The Savior finds His way.
        Christmas is come!

To lighted hearths whose fires make silver linings
    Behind the day's dark cloud,
To halls where Beauty's light is shining,
    Where dancers laugh and crowd,
        Christmas is come!

"Long love, long peace and reconciliation,"
    We sing aloud, and then,
Their tones grown strong with joy and exultation,
    The great bells chime, Amen!
        Christmas is come!

Milwaukee Sentinel, December 25, 1868

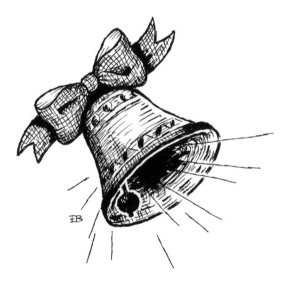

Holiday Musings

by Edna Meudt 1906-1989

Tree, tissue garlands, and bell set the stage. Like minutiae held in amber, the scene speaks yesteryear. We who remember are sad— for the sake of Christmas, for childhood homes that fantasy makes into lovely abodes of peace. The language of love is changeless, if not forever.

Read first the serious mother concerned with candlelight and fire, weary of Christmas-making realities: cleaning, baking, popcorn stringing, boxed secrets, decorations hung in the locked room. Anticlimactic now, this solemnity of a family portrait. *When I said, "I love you," did I think we would always be like we were, carefree as colts gamboling in pasture? I knew there would be duties, but I am so tired!*

The handsome father knows directions. He works at planning/ dreaming. (Fulfillment is seldom happenstance.) *A fine Christmas! What more could a man ask than to be able to give to those he loves? My darling likes best the ebony, monogrammed dresser set, I think. Our son, his quadricycle. The Gramophone and disks were more than we can afford. But a home needs music.*

Look into the time machine. What else do you see? There on the floor, a peaceable kingdom—the circus wagon opened wide for the lion to visit the barn. Tin soldiers at attention. The budding boy not fully enlightened to opportunity. (Next year he will ask for a *real* pony.) The little-girl-loved, a miniature woman. Her dolls in disarray, her carriage, tea set, games, and picture books abandoned as befits the occasion. *When the picture is made, they will see I'm just as pretty as my mama.*

Oh, look again. Multicolored wax candles light this room, multiplied shadows crisscross each other over the walls. The Christmas tree becomes a golden ark lifting its happiness-load against the darkness. It rocks on time's stream only as long as we place an evergreen in a public building and light our own outdoor trees.

Every age is equidistant from eternity. They, as we, accepted the tinsel tarnish, broken baubles, doubts, the merchant exacting his price. We, as they, walk the way of discovery. Sooner or later we come to understand Good Friday and Easter because we, too, suffer, triumph, lose. Getting to Bethlehem is more difficult. One must love to get there. The season for travel is short, and the heart of Christmas is distant as the star.

ACKNOWLEDGMENTS

"Snowfall in Childhood" by Ben Hecht from *Esquire* Magazine, Nov. 1934. Copyright © Ben Hecht. Used with permission.

"Slowing Down" from *A Cabin in the Woods* by Jerry Apps. Copyright © Argus Corporation. Used with permission.

"Long Journey through Wisconsin by Sleigh" from *Memoirs of Father Mazzuchetti* O.P.

"Christmastide, Lake Michigan" from *Old Fonts and Real Folks* by Susan Burdick Davis. Used with permission.

Cranberry selections from *Autobiography of a Winnebago Indian Woman* by Mountain Wolf Woman. N.W. Lurie, editor. Copyright © 1961, University of Michigan Press. Used with permission. Also from *Flavor of Wisconsin* by Harva Hacten. Wisconsin Historical Society Press. Used with permission.

"Christmas on the Range" from *Portraits* by Daniel Berrigan. Used with permission.

"The Christmas Program" by Dolores Curran from *Yarns of Wisconsin*. Copyright © 1978. Used with permission.

"The Play's the Thing" from *A Nostalgic Almanac* by Edna Houg. Copyright © 1980, Augsburg Publishing House. Used with permission.

"Rascal at Christmas" from *Rascal, A Memoir of a Better Era* by Sterling North. Copyright © 1963, E. P. Dutton and Co. Used with permission.

"The Christmas Costume" from *Magical Melons* by Carol Ryrie Brink. Published by the MacMillan Co. Used with permission.

"Memories of Christmas at the Wade House" from the diary of Jennie Hamilton Root. Used with permission of the Wisconsin State Historical Society, Greenbush.

"Christmas Tree" from *Crunching Gravel* by Robert Peters. Used with permission.